A
TOR
DOUBLE
ACTION
WESTERN

Zane Grey

THE KIDNAPPING OF COLLIE YOUNGER

OUTLAWS OF PALOUSE

A TOM DOHERTY ASSOCIATES BOOK
NEW YORK

This is a work of fiction. All the characters and events portrayed in this book are fictitious, and any resemblance to real people or events is purely coincidental.

THE KIDNAPPING OF COLLIE YOUNGER

OUTLAWS OF PALOUSE

A Tor Book
Published by Tom Doherty Associates, Inc.
49 West 24th Street
New York, N.Y. 10010

Cover art by Stan Borak

ISBN: 0-812-51617-6

First edition: June 1991

Printed in the United States of America

0 9 8 7 6 5 4 3 2 1

THE KIDNAPPING OF COLLIE YOUNGER

·1·

It was Collie Younger who dared the picnic gang to go in swimming. This girl from Texas had been the gayest and the wildest of last June's graduates of Hazelton Normal College; and as on many former occasions, her audacity had been infectious. But despite the warm September sun the water of Canyon Creek would be icy. Frost had long since come to tinge the oaks and aspens of that high Arizona altitude. It was one thing to bask in the golden sunshine and gaze into the amber water, which reflected the red walls, the fringed ledges, the colored sycamore leaves floating down, and quite another to plunge into it.

"You're a lot of daid ones," taunted Collie, with a shake of her bright head. "This picnic is a flop. The boys are playing poker. It's hot down heah. Me for a swim!"

"But, Collie, we did not bring any bathing suits," remonstrated Sara Brecken.

"We don't need any."

"You wouldn't—"

"Shore I would—if we went up the creek in the shade. But it's nice and sunny heah. We can keep something on and dry off pronto."

"I'm for it," cried Helen Bender, mischievously. "Anything to shock these boys out of their poker game!"

That settled the argument. Sara reluctantly followed her six companions down off the green bench to the huge rocks that lined the shore. Collie was the first to emerge from behind them into the open.

Roddy Brecken, who never had any money to gamble with and no luck besides, sat watching the red-sided trout shining in the crystal water. Espying Collie in her scant attire and slim allurement he drew up with a start and a sharp breath. He had never seen such an apparition. In town, the couple of times he had encountered her since his return to Hazelton, she had appeared a pretty girl in a crowd of prettier ones. But this was different. Half naked, she was not so small; her form had more roundness than anyone would have guessed; her graceful arms and legs held a warm tint of fading tan; and as she gingerly stuck a small foot into the water she leaped up with a shriek and a toss of her shining curls. Then, at the bantering of the girls emerging from behind the rocks, Collie daringly dove into the pool. She bobbed up splashing and blowing, to call out in a half-strangled voice: "Come—on in.... Water's—great."

Roddy had arisen to make tracks away from there, as soon as he could unrivet his feet. But his retreat was checked by the spectacle of the six girls hurrying over the rocks. It appeared to Roddy that his gaze took in a great deal of uncovered white flesh. The girls made haste to wade in and submerge their charms.

Their squealing laughing melee broke up the poker game. The other six boys came trooping down, headed by Roddy's brother John, upon whose handsome face the expression of amazement was displaced by one of disapproval and annoyance. The other young men did not take the scene amiss.

"I'm ararin' to go," yelled Bruce Jones.

"Let's pile in, fellers, as we are," suggested another.

"Don't be a lot of fools! Not for mine. The sun will soon drop behind the wall."

John Brecken's vigorous opposition to the idea did not deter two of the boys from joining the girls in the water. But the impromptu bathing was obviously destined to a very short duration. John might have spared his peremptory call for his sister Sara to come out. Presently all of them, except Collie, made for the shore, and if they had looked outrageous before they went in, Roddy wondered what words could be used to describe them now. The boys ran puffing up the rocks. "I'll say—it wa-was—c-cold," declared Bruce, making for an isolated place in the sun. The girls, huddling together, slopped out of sight into their retreat. Collie kept swimming and splashing about. Roddy conceived an idea she was doing it to annoy John.

"Collie Younger, you come right out of there," yelled John. "You'll catch your death."

"Cold water's good for me. Cools me off," replied the girl.

"Yes, and your hair will look fine tonight for the dance."

That clever sally had the desired effect. But Collie did not bother to wade around back of the rocks, like the other girls. She boldly climbed up at the point where she had plunged off.

"You're a sight," declared John, whipping off his coat, and making toward her.

"What for? Sore eyes?"

John's vehement denial was at distinct variance with Roddy's rapt attention. The beauty and the daring of the girl were potent enough to counteract his resentment at her impertinence to John and an underlying disapproval of her lack of modesty.

"Yeah? Well, you don't have to look at me," rejoined Collie, flippantly.

"Here. Put this on."

"I don't want your coat."

"Collie!—You look—like—like hell!

"Jealous, Big Boy? You would be. I'll bet if you and I were heah alone you wouldn't register such absurd objection."

"I won't have this," sputtered Brecken.

"*You* won't. Since when were you my boss? Jack, I'm fed up on you. We're not engaged, and even if we were, I'd do as I pleased."

"You bet you would," said John, bitterly. "You get a kick out of such indecent display—"

"Who's indecent?" queried Collie, hotly. "It's your mind, Jack Brecken. Shut up—or I'll drop what I've got on and go in again."

John flung his coat upon her and wheeled in high dudgeon to climb up on the bench, where the boys teased him good-humoredly. Roddy preferred to leave his perch on the rock and saunter up the creek under the trees.

It seemed good to get back to Arizona, to which he had returned only infrequently during the last few years. Canyon Creek had been one of Roddy's haunts as a boy, and the dry smell of pine, the stream rushing here in white wreaths about the mossy rocks, and eddying there in amber pools, where the big trout lay like shadows, brought back memories and dreams that hurt. What days he and John had spent together in these woods. Red squirrels chattered into the still solitude of the forested canyon. He encountered deer tracks in the dust of the trail. What a joy it would be to again take a fall hunt with John. The smoky haze in the glades, the brooding melancholy of the canyon, the plaintive murmur of insects, the intervals of unbroken solemn silence assured Roddy that the hunting season was not many weeks away.

He retraced his steps, sorry to leave the shade of the gray-barked sycamores, reluctant to join the crowd of young people again. The boys were all Arizonians, whom he had always known, but the girls, except Sara, were strangers from beyond Hazelton. Roddy had noted with an unwonted stir of feeling that his bad reputation had in no wise kept them aloof. In fact it had seemed quite the opposite. The Texas girl, who had made such an exhibition of herself, had cast too many glances in Roddy's direction for him to believe them casual. No doubt she was taking John down the line, and would do the same thing to him if she had the opportunity. He felt sorry for John, who was so obviously in love with her. And to feel sorry for John, to whom he had always looked up, was not a pleasant sensation.

But what eyes that girl had! He had thought they were hazel until he had seen them this day, as she stood bareheaded in the sunlight, and then he decided they were topaz. Their color could not have had anything to do with their tantalizing expression. And he admitted that the rest of her matched her eyes.

Roddy fell ill at ease. He had not wanted to attend this picnic with John, who however had insisted until he gave in. Absence and a gradual drifting, had not changed his boyhood love for his brother. That, Roddy reflected, had been the only anchor he had known.

When he got back to the others the sun had gone down behind the fringe of the western rim. Deep shadows showed under the walls. The warm breath moving up the canyon had cooled. Roddy's last glance at the creek took in the green-gold sycamore leaves floating downstream.

The boys were packing baskets and coats to the cars parked some distance away. John, looking sombre and with traces of his anger still on his face, stood apart, evidently waiting for Collie. It developed, however, that he was waiting for Roddy. "Collie's riding back with Bruce and Sara," he said. "I'm glad of that, for it'll give me a chance to talk to you. Let's rustle."

Nevertheless John slowed up as soon as he drew Roddy away from the others. He had something on his mind and apparently found breaching it not so easy.

"Rod, my mind's been simmering ever since you came home," he began, presently. "This break of Collie's today brought it to a boil. I told you I was simply nuts over her, didn't I?"

"Yes. But you needn't have told me. Anyone could see that."

"Is that so?—Well, she has been playing fast and loose with me. I'm sure Collie cares most for me, else she wouldn't . . . but she plays with the other boys, too, and it's got my goat. I'll simply have to throw a bridle on her. . . . Once my wife, she'd be all right."

"Brother, I reckon what you need on her is a hackamore," observed Roddy, with a laugh.

They reached the glade through which the road ran. The cars were leaving. Roddy saw Collie's face flash out of the last one, as she bent a curious glance back at them. On second thought Roddy decided Collie had looked back at him. John might not have been there at all.

"I'll tell the world," admitted John, grimly, "I'm at the end of my rope. And if the plan I have fails—or if you refuse to do it—I'm sunk."

"Me!—Refuse?" ejaculated Roddy, in amazement. "For Pete's sake, what could *I* do?"

"You can kidnap her, by thunder, and scare her half to death."

For a moment, Roddy stared at his brother, waiting for him to give an indication that he was joking. But John's face remained deadly serious. "Well," John finally remarked impatiently, "did you get what I said?"

"Jack, are you crazy?" Roddy finally ejaculated. "You must have it bad. Nothing doing!"

"Wait till you hear my proposition," went on John, white and tense. "Listen. . . . Roddy, Dad left all his property to us, fifty-fifty. You hate the store and you'd never stick there long at a time. I've run the business, improved it, made money, I've given and sent you money every time you asked for it. I didn't begrudge it. I know how you feel about living in town. I've tried to understand you—sympathize with you. Some of your scrapes the last two years have been hard for me to swallow and have given you a bad reputation."

"Jack, I haven't been so hot," replied Roddy, dropping his head, ashamed, yet grateful to John for not being harsher.

"Well, I propose to buy you out. Will you sell? It would be better for the business."

"I'd jump at it, Jack."

"Fine. I'll give you five thousand, half down, and my half share in old Middleton's cattle and range. That property had run down. It's not worth much now. But it can be worked into a good paying business. The old fellow won't last long. That property would eventually be yours. A ranch in the Verdi, where there's forest left and game!"

"Right down my alley, Jack," returned Roddy, with feeling. "I know the range. Swell! But I'd forgotten you had thrown in with Middleton.... What's the string to this proposition?"

"Do you like it?"

"So far it's great. And darn fair of you, Jack."

"All right. Here's the string. I've been thinking this over for some time. I want you to kidnap Collie—drive her down under the Tonto Rim to that old cabin in Turkey Canyon. Treat her rough. I don't care a damn how mean you are to her, so long as you make yourself out to be plenty tough. Scare hell out of her. As it turns out we can easily keep the kidnapping a secret. We'll plan for me to trail you—find you on a certain date. Collie will be subdued—worn out with mistreatment and hard fare and fright—then I'll come along to rescue her."

For a moment Roddy felt an impulse to laugh. This could be nothing but a bad joke of John's. But in John's face was no suggestion of humor and his voice was anxious and urgent. Almost pityingly Roddy asked, "Jack Brecken, do you figure she'll fall for you—then?"

"I hope she will. If that doesn't fetch her nothing will—the contrary little flirt!"

"But, man alive! She's from Texas. She's a live wire. She'd kill you if she found it out. And I reckon she'd kill me anyhow."

"Yes, Collie will be game. It's a risk. But I've *got* to do it."

"How on earth could I get away with it? She's popular—has lots of friends. They'd raise hell."

"Ordinarily, yes. But this deal has been made

for me. Listen . . . Collie graduated last spring. But she stayed on all summer, until now. She's leaving for Texas tomorrow. I've offered to drive her over to Colton to catch the main line express. All the girls will be busy or in school when I call for her. She'll say good-bye to them at the dance tonight. She intends to stop off at Albuquerque to visit an uncle for two weeks. And she'll not wire him till she gets on the train. I'll send you in my old car, in which you'll pack grub, blankets, etc. You'll whisk her away—and at a time we'll set, I'll drive down to Turkey Canyon to get her."

"Just like that!" ejaculated Roddy, snapping his fingers.

"Will you do it?" demanded John, tersely.

"I'm afraid I'll have to turn it down. . . . I'd do almost anything for you, Jack. And if that kid has doublecrossed you I could shake the gizzards out of her, but—but—"

"Why won't you?"

"Jack, it's so—so—hell! I don't know what. So ridiculous! And even if we could get away with it, it seems a dirty trick to pull on any girl—even if she has played you for a sucker. You can't really love her."

"I'm crazy about Collie. And I tell you again if you fail me I'll be sunk. And don't forget my offer of the money and ranch." John's tone was verging on despair.

"Money doesn't cut much ice with me. But that Verdi ranch—I could go for that in a big way," cogitated Roddy.

"Well, here's your change to get it, along with money to make it a fine thing for you. A place to settle down. You could quit this rolling-stone stuff. There'll always be good hunting and fishing in the Verdi. Why, that canyon runs down into the Tonto Basin."

"Sounds great, Jack," said Roddy, gripping the car with a strong brown hand. "Only—the girl part is the deal—that sticks in my craw."

"I don't see why. Listen, Rod! There's something coming to Collie Younger. She needs taming. I should think it'd appeal to you."

"Well, it doesn't," denied Roddy forcibly. But the instant his words were spent he realized they were false. And that astonished him. The idea intrigued him—took hold of him. Suddenly a picture of Collie flashed into mind—her rebellious face and challenging eyes, as she had walked unashamed and free, like a young goddess out of her bath. That picture proved devastating. Then he sensed a resentment towards this high-stepping Texas kid and an urge to avenge her trifling with his blundering brother, who had never had any luck with girls. All the same it looked like a crowning folly for him.

"Sorry, old man. I just can't see it your way," he said, and got into the car. John violently slammed the door shut and took the wheel. His state of mind might have been judged by his reckless driving up a steep and narrow road to the rim. Roddy gazed across the deep canyon, now full of blue shadows, to the long sweep of the cedared desert toward the west. Purple clouds burned with a ruddy fire, low down along the horizon. To the south, towards the Verdi, the canyon wound its snake-like trail of red and gold into the green wilderness. Facing northward, as John headed the car homeward, Roddy viewed the huge bulk of the mountains looming high, crowned with white. How hard to leave this Arizona range again!

John drove like a man possessed of devils and roared past the other cars halfway to Hazelton. Dusk had fallen when he reached home in the outskirts of town. Then he broke the silence. "Rod," he said, "you may have changed. Once you were full of the Old Nick. But if sentiment and romance are dead in you, look at my offer as simply business."

"Jack, I'm no good. All the same I'd hate to pull a low-down stunt like that."

"You're not acquainted with Collie. She'd get a kick out of being kidnapped."

"Why don't you kidnap her yourself?"

"I would. But I figured it wouldn't work. It takes time and besides I haven't an excuse to leave the business just now. The rescue act would be much better, and I'd be more of a hero in her eyes. Collie's a Southerner, brimfull of romance. She's crazy over the movies. Goes to every picture. Once she told me she could fall for me much quicker if I did something heroic. That's what gave me this idea."

"That may be okay with you, Jack. But somehow it doesn't persuade me. She's spunky, and she won't be be bossed. I'd say that was your great fault, Jack."

"I like my own way and I see that I get it. I've set my heart on Collie, the little fiend."

John's words smacked of arrogance, but Roddy could sense the panic behind them.

"But this deal of yours isn't on the level," rejoined Roddy, curtly.

"Neither is Collie on the level."

"Oh, she isn't!" Roddy stared aghast.

"Not with men, that's a cinch. In the two years she has gone to college here, she has taken every fellow I know down the line. Cowboys are her especial dish. She swears she adores them. But I noticed none of them lasted long."

"Well. It'd depend on how far she—"

"I don't know. But there have been times when

I was so jealous and sick I wanted to murder her. Then she'd be sweeter to me than ever."

"Jack I should think you'd be leery of such a girl—for a wife."

John waved that statement aside. "Come to the Normal dance tonight. See for yourself. She'll make a play for you. I got that today. You're husky and handsome. She's heard gossip about you. She's curious."

"But I haven't a decent suit to my back," protested Roddy.

"I'll lend you one. My clothes always fit you."

"If my reputation is so bad, I should think—"

"That will make you all the more interesting." There was a tinge of bitterness in John's voice. "Besides, Normal dances are always short of men. Everybody in town will be invited. All the cowboys on the range. It'll be the first dance of the season and sure a swell affair."

John's importunity weighed powerfully on Roddy. Moreover he grew conscious of a curious eagerness to see Collie Younger again. He gave in to it. And he had a stubborn conception of his own about that girl—a something born from the scornful flash of topaz eyes at his brother.

Roddy accepted John's brand-new dark suit and dressed himself with a growing amusement and interest. After dinner he walked up to town. The cold night wind whipped down from the black peaks. Roddy wished for a fleece-lined coat, such as he used to wear while riding. For the first time since his arrival home he strolled into poolrooms and hotel lobbies, curious about whom he might meet. No lack of old acquaintances and some sundry drinks of hard liquor warmed Roddy into a heartening mood. He fell in with some cowboys and went to the dance with them.

The Normal College was an institution that had

been established since Roddy's school days in Hazelton. He had never been inside the big building, which was situated a little way out of town in a grove of pine trees. The several hundred automobiles parked all around attested to a large attendance at the dance. Reluctant to go in, and thinking it best to walk to and fro a while in the cold air, Roddy gave his eager cowboys comrades the slip.

When he did enter the building he experienced a pleasant surprise at sight of the many pretty girls in formal gowns, and clean-cut western boys with tanned faces, talking and laughing at the entrance to the colorfully decorated ballroom. A forgotten something stirred in his veins. It swelled with the sudden burst of tantalizing music which drowned the low murmur of voices. Roddy found himself carried along with the crowd into the big hall.

Roddy took to the sidelines, intending to find enjoyment watching the dancers. He quite forgot his reason for coming. But he had scarcely had a moment to himself when a gracious woman, evidently one of the hostesses, swooped down upon him and led him off. To Roddy's dismay he saw a whole contingent of girls in white and pink and blue, all apparently eager-eyed for a partner. Before he realized what it was all about he found himself on the floor with a dark-haired girl. He was awkward and he stepped on her feet. Mortified by this, Roddy woke up to exert all his wit and memory to recall a once skilful lightness of foot and accommodations to rhythm. He had begun to dance creditably when the music stopped.

One after another, then, he was given four partners, the last of whom was a decidedly comely girl whose auburn-tinted head came up to his shoulder. With her Roddy started out well. But anyone save a cripple could have danced with this girl, Roddy assured himself.

"Don't you know me, Roddy?" she asked, presently, roguishly.

"Indeed, no. I'm sorry. Ought I?"

"Hardly. I've grown up and changed."

"Did I go to school with you?"

"Yes. But I was a kid in the first grade. I'm Jessie Evans."

"Jessie Evans? . . . You couldn't be that long-legged, freckle-faced, red-headed little imp who used to . . . ?"

"You've got my number, Roddy," she replied, gayly.

"No?—Well, of all things! You, little Jessie, grown into such—such a stunning girl?"

"Thanks. It's nice of you to say so."

Roddy got along delightfully with Jessie and graduated into something of his old ease at dancing. He did not realize at all what a fine time he was having until after that dance, when he encountered his brother and several of the picnic party. Then he remembered, and went to some pains to conceal his self-consciousness.

"Rod, I see you're stepping right out," remarked John, amiably. Manifestly he was in good spirits, and looked very handsome with his strong dark face minus its brooding anger. Something had cheered Jack up. No doubt it was the bewitching little girl who clung to his arm.

"Howdy, Jack. Sure, I'm enjoying myself," replied Roddy. Then he bowed to Collie and the others.

"I'm glad, old man. It's good to see you here," said John, and his heartiness seemed free of any ulterior interest in Roddy's presence. "You must dance with Collie. Here, take her for the next."

"I'd be delighted—if she'll risk it."

"Is there any great risk?" drawled the Texas girl, looking up with her penetrating topaz eyes. She wore a gown that matched them and her hair. Her rounded arms and neck, almost as gold of hue as her gown, brought back strikingly to Roddy the picture of her that he could never forget.

"I'm a rotten dancer."

"You cain't be any worse than some of these hoofers heah," she rejoined lifting her little hands to him as the music started. In a moment he felt as if he were holding a fairy. He responded to the stimulus by dancing better than he ever had before. When they got halfway round the hall she said:

"Roddy, you're not a rotten dancer. But you'd do better to hold me closer. Not at arm's length!"

"I'm a tenderfoot—at dancing," he replied, apologetically, but he tightened his clasp.

"Yeah? I hadn't noticed it. But I'd prefer that to these boys who dance so darn well they cain't do anything else."

Collie inspired as well as intoxicated Roddy. It was impossible not to take advantage of her suggestion. Then he felt her as substantial as she had looked that afternoon. Her curly fragrant head rested low upon his shoulder. She clung to him without in the least hampering his step.

"Roddy, you didn't approve of me this afternoon—down in the Canyon Creek?"

"I—how . . . what makes you think that?" he stammered.

"The way you looked at me. Maybe I did go too far—before a stranger, anyhow. But Jack gives me a pain in the neck."

"You give him a worse pain than that," said Roddy, with a laugh. "There! I got out of step. Collie, I can't talk and dance."

"All right. But tell me what you thought—about me—this afternoon."

"Well, I didn't get beyond how pretty you looked."

"Oh! . . . Not so poor, Roddy." She did not speak again until the dance ended.

"Come, let's beat it outdoors," she commanded, and dragged him from the ballroom. "Pinch somebody's coat or wrap. I'm a Southerner, you know. I love your Arizonie, but oh, it freezes me to death."

They went out under the giant pines. White gowns shone in the moonlight. Other couples passed them going in. It was wonderful out there despite the cold. Black and star-crowned, the peaks pierced the dark blue sky.

"You're not much of a talker, are you?" inquired Collie.

"Me? Gosh, no. I haven't any line," replied Roddy.

"Not much! You cain't fool this dame. . . . I wish you had come back heah a year ago."

"Why?"

"Then I could have known you. I leave Hazelton tomorrow and I won't be back for a while. We might not meet again."

"I reckon you're not missing much."

Collie gave his arm a squeeze. "Don't be so modest, old dear," she replied.

They came to a huge fallen pine that stretched across the campus. "Lift me up," said the girl. Roddy put his hands under her arms and sailed her aloft to a perch on the log.

"How strong you are!" she murmured, as she smoothed down her gown. Her head was now on a level with his. The moonlight silvered her hair and worked magic in her eyes and enhanced the charm of her face.

"I've been cowboy, miner, lumber jack," he said, lightly. "All professions that require strength."

"I've heard that you were a hard drinker, gambler, fighter—in fact a hard nut."

"I seem to have a good reputation."

"Is it true?"

"True? I reckon so."

"I wonder. . . . Roddy, you're the best-looking fellow I've met heah. And you've a nicer manner than most. You remind me of a Southerner."

"My granddad was from Texas. My mother from Missouri. That's south, you know."

"Are you staying long heah?"

"I reckon not. I cain't stay anyplace long. Why do you ask?"

"Oh, I told you I was coming back," she returned, with a flash of her eyes.

"But what about John? I gathered you and he had been pretty friendly."

"Oh, John's sort of dotty about me and I thought I was in love with him. But he's too slow for me and too bossy so I'm going to give him the gate." There was an insolence in the girl's tone that antagonized Roddy.

"Does Jack suspect that?" he asked, wishing to lead her on.

"Not a chance. He couldn't believe it. Says I don't know my mind two days running."

"He appeared happy tonight."

"I made up with him—kissed him. If I hadn't done so, this last night heah would have flopped. I wanted to enjoy it. . . . I'm enjoying it very much—right now."

"Are you going to tell him?"

"Yes, in the mawning. Maybe I'll string him along till later. It'd be fun to do it at the train."

Her mocking high-pitched laughter pealed out.

Her eyes danced in the moonlight. That was the moment Roddy understood his brother and accepted his offer. To tame this imperious and ruthless young lady appealed to all that was wild and reckless in Roddy. Aligned with his loyalty to John, it set the balance.

"Jack asked me to drive you across to Colton," said Roddy, smoothly. "He's a Mason, you know, and has an important conference."

"He did?—How jolly. I'm tickled pink," she cried, ecstatically.

"When and where shall I call for you?"

"The cottage where I've been living with Helen and Mary is on Oak Street, right next to the women's dormitory. Do you know where that is?"

"Yes. What time?"

"Two o'clock sharp."

"Baggage?"

"Plenty. But no trunks. I'll have the bags taken out."

"Okay."

"It's a nice long ride over. I hated the idea of Jack driving me. He's so businesslike about everything he does and he cain't enjoy the scenery. If we leave at two we'll have plenty of time. You don't want to hurry, do you?"

"Reckon I'll creep along, if you like."

"Then we can talk, too, and plan. . . . I'm not saying good-bye forever. . . . You'll write to me. . . . Roddy if I was staying on heah, I'd fall for you something awful."

"Oh, yeah? Lucky you're not.

"For me—or you, darling?"

"You. I'm a bad hombre, Collie."

"So I've heahed. Wild guy—devil with the women. And you haven't even squeezed my hand. Pooh! That's a lot of baloney."

They walked back to the school building, and sought out John who was standing alone. Roddy gave his brother a significant look.

"I told Collie that you wanted me to drive her over to the main line," he informed John, "and she decided she could trust me."

It was lucky that Collie was looking at Roddy, for such a flood of relief and gratification passed over John's features that Collie would have suspected something had she seen his expression.

Before John could answer, Roddy turned to Collie. "So long, Collie, see you at two tomorrow," he said, and walked off into the moonlight.

He had let himself in for it, he mused rather grimly. But the girl had it coming to her. She was an outrageous flirt, and had tried to do to him as she had done to John, and undoubtedly to numbers of other boys. She needed a lesson, a severe one, and it seemed that he, Roddy, was the one chosen to give it. There was a strange satisfaction in that thought.

Then his doubt set in again. After all, what business was it of his? Why shouldn't John carry out his own crazy plans. What had induced him, Roddy, to give in to the idea? When he came to think of it, no one but the girl herself, with her provocative ways. He was a softy and she was taking him down the line just as she had taken John. It wasn't a sane thing to do, and he was damned if he'd carry it out. He'd go right straight to John and tell him it was impossible.

Roddy turned and started back under the trees. Just as he was about to mount the steps of the school building, a movement in the shrubbery at the side drew his attention. The moonlight flooded down on the tantalizing face of Collie and on the white arms that were creeping around the neck of a cowboy Roddy had never before seen.

Roddy's right-about-face was so swift that he almost lost his balance. "You win, John," he muttered to himself. "I'll go through with it!"

• 2 •

NEXT DAY, THE LAST OF RODDY'S MANY ERRANDS WAS to drive to the bank to cash the check for twenty-five hundred dollars that John had forced on him, along with the papers of a transfer of his share in Middleton's ranch. John had not been taking any chances of Roddy's flunking on his part of the bargain.

The teller did not have so large an amount of cash in the cage and had to send to the vault for it. "Can't use checks in the country I'm going to," John explained. "I'm not known and anyway the backswoodsmen don't believe in checks."

"Well, be careful," the teller warned him. "There are always shady characters hanging around."

John laughed and pocketed his bills. "I'll be on the lookout," he assured the man.

It was after two o'clock when Roddy turned in the direction of the women's dormitory. He stepped on the gas to go tearing across the railroad track ahead of a freight train. And in less than two minutes he was passing the noisy sawmill, with its great cloud of creamy smoke rolling aloft, to sight the college building beyond. In another moment he spied Collie at the gate of a small cottage. His heart leaped. All day the adventure had been unreal till he saw her. As he slowed to a stop he observed there did not appear to be anyone but Collie in sight. She looked very smart in a brown suit and carried a coat on her arm. A pile of suitcases and bags lay on the sidewalk.

"Howdy, Texas. Sorry to be late," said Roddy, as he leaped out. "Hop in the front seat."

"Oh, Roddy, I thought you'd never come," she cried, giving him a radiant smile. "I see stingy Jack gave you his old car. What's all the junk?"

"I reckon I'll need to be alone in the woods for a while—after this ride with you. So I'm going camping," replied Roddy, and he began to throw her bags into the back of the car. As he slipped in to the wheel he looked around to see if anyone was observing them. There were no pedestrians but a car was raising dust at the railroad crossing. Roddy drove rapidly toward the open country. The deed was done.

Collie edged closer to him and hooked a little hand under his arm. Excited and thrilled, evidently, she had not noted that they were travelling in the wrong direction.

"Oh, swell!" she ejaculated. "I'm tired. Had only three hours' sleep," and with a sigh she sank against him. But she kept on talking, about the dance, about the girls—about Jack, and how she hated to leave Arizona.

Roddy was too excited to pay much attention to her chatter, but he could not help but be affected by the softness and warmth of her person. At his lack of response Collie presently remarked dryly that she hoped he was going to make the ride interesting.

"I'll tell the world," he assured her. In the little mirror he caught sight of a car gaining from behind. Roddy did not intend to allow anyone to see Collie, let alone pass him, and accordingly he increased the speed.

"Collie, how'd you like to have me drive you clear to Albuquerque," he queried, daringly.

"Wonderful!" she burst out, in amaze and delight. "But how long would you take—where would we—"

"A couple of days, loafing along. Chance for us to get acquainted."

"Say, Big Boy, you're doing pretty well. . . . Where'd we sleep?"

"I'd make a bed for you in the back seat. I have blankets and pillows. I'll sleep on the ground."

"Can we get away with it?"

"Cinch. We'd roll through the few towns there are. Camp in lonesome places. I brought grub, fruit, everything, and I can cook."

She leaned against him, silent for a long moment. Then she asked: "Can I trust you, Roddy?"

"I reckon it'll be risky," he replied, with a laugh.

"Well, I'll take the chance! It'll be a lark—my last in Arizona. . . . Okay, Roddy."

Roddy was hindered from making a ready response to her immediate acceptance of his proposal. Her tone, when she had asked if she could trust him, scarcely savored of heedlessness; it had contained a note foreign to every other thing she had said to him. It gave him pause.

Roddy happened at the moment to glance into his rear-sight mirror, and found that the car behind was coming up fast. Then accelerating his speed, he turned a corner, only to be confronted by a bad stretch of road that would be hazardous to fast travel. He decided to let the car pass, if it caught him before the narrow strip ended.

"Slide down, Collie, so that driver can't see you."

"Gee!" ejaculated the girl, gleefully. "We're starting off well."

The approaching automobile was an old Ford with two occupants. They came on apace and were almost up with Roddy when he reached a wider spot where they might have passed him. They did not, however, make the attempt, until just at the end of the rough stretch, when they astounded Roddy with a honking rush.

It angered him. Instead of swerving he hit into high speed. And at that instant the front of the Ford shot into sight alongside.

"Stop, that!" came the hoarse bellow. *"An' stick 'em up!"*

Roddy went cold all over. The rattling car rocked almost abreast of him. A man leaned out back of the windshield, automatic gun extended. His ham-shaped visage, with pointed chin covered by a reddish beard, seemed vaguely familiar. Somewhere, that very day, Roddy had seen it. In a flash Roddy stepped his car to its limit. As he forged ahead, there came a crash of splintered glass accompanied by a gun-shot. His left side-shield had been hit by a bullet. A fierce indistinguishable command to stop filled Roddy's ears. He slid down in his seat as far as he dared, yelling to Collie to keep hidden, and drove on, the cold shock to his internals giving way to the heat of anger. A holdup! Where had he seen that man? Every second he stingingly expected another shot and bullet. But it did not come. This old touring car of John's simply swallowed up the road. Walls of green flashed by on each side. Presently Roddy dared to look back. Already he was farther from the pursuing car than he had imagined. Almost out of range! Perhaps the holdup man had shot to halt him, without murderous intent. Roddy sat up and drove as never before in his life, and presently he had left his pursuers far behind and finally out of sight around a bend.

"Sit up, Collie. We showed him our heels."

She came up as if for air: "G-gangsters?"

"Search me. But that guy with the gun looked plenty tough. *Where* did I see him?"

"Step on it, Roddy."

"I was doing seventy back aways. Sixty now. This old bus can go some. . . . Collie, that little play wasn't on the program."

"You ought to pack a gun," declared this young lady from Texas.

"I've got two in the car. But gosh! I never thought of them. . . . Where in hell—now. . . . By thunder! *The bank.* It was in the bank where I saw that lantern-jawed hombre. I went in to cash Jack's check. He saw me with the money. . . . Well, what do you know about that!"

"They'll trail us. And this country is getting wilder. Oh, I should have made you drive me to the train!"

"Too late now, Collie," he replied, grimly, and he meant that in several senses.

Roddy slowed to a reasonable speed. He did not trust the car to hold together. The road was good and he had now no fear of being caught. The fences failed, and gradually the slashed area where the timber had been cut off. Patches of goldenrod blazed among the sagebrush under the pines. Presently he passed the forks of the road, where a signboard marked the branch that turned west down to Canyon Creek.

"Canyon Creek!" exclaimed Collie. "Why, that's the road we took yesterday!"

"You're not liable to forget it—or this road either."

"This road, I've been on it. We drove down to the Natural Bridge a year and more ago. . . . Roddy, it runs to the left of Canyon Creek, and that canyon gets deeper all the way. It's a terribly cut-up country. How'll we ever cross that canyon?"

"We can't."

"But we've got to go east. We'll be farther and farther out of our way."

"Shall I turn back?"

"Oh, no. We cain't do that with those bums chasing us."

"There's a road which turns off to the west, down here at Long Valley. It goes to Wilcox. We can take that. But then we'll have to go back through Hazelton."

"No. We'll keep on and drive way around somehow. A day or so more won't make any great difference. . . . I'm scared yet, but I'll soon get a kick out of it."

Stretches of rocky cedared desert alternated with straggling pine forest. Collie lapsed into thoughtful quiet and again leaned upon Roddy's shoulder. Once he felt her studying his face. Was she beginning to wonder? It was all one to Roddy, for she would soon learn of his nefarious design. They passed a ranch zone, poor range, sparsely grassed, and scarce in cattle. The depression had hit these ranchers as well as town folk. Beyond, they climbed into forest country again, passed through bare spots where in spring there were weedy ponds, and so on to the lake and cottages of Hazelton's summer resort. It appeared deserted now. Collie was asleep with heavy head slipping low on Roddy's shoulder when he drove by the lake.

Beyond this point Roddy seldom looked back. He had not thought, however, that the holdup men would abandon the pursuit. On that dusty road they could trail him as long as he stayed on it. There followed a twenty-five mile stretch that ate up an hour of hard driving. Circling Snow Lake he passed on through the woods to Crooked Valley.

This was where he had to turn to the left from the main highway into the forest. And he needed to do so without being seen by any of the people who lived there. Moreover, he did not want to leave any tracks into the forester's road that led down to Turkey Canyon. Selecting a grove well carpeted with pine-needles, Roddy drove to the right, off under the pines, as far from the highway as level ground permitted.

Darkness was coming on apace. When he stopped, the jolt of the car awakened Collie. She sat up bewildered, her curls all awry. "Night!— Where the heck am I? Gee, what a lonesome place!"

Roddy explained that he had thought it best to hide here until their pursuers went by. He advised her to get out and stretch her legs while he unpacked something to eat and drink. After that he would make room for her to sleep on the back seat. Here in the woods it was much warmer than out driving on the road. He concluded to get along without a fire, but did not hesitate to use his flashlight.

When presently he was ready to walk back to the road to watch till the Ford went by Collie said: "Roddy, I'm not stuck on staying heah alone. Let me go with you."

"Stay in the car. This is no picnic," he replied, and his tone was gruff.

Collie's eyes flashed and she retorted spiritedly: "Well, you needn't be so huffy about it."

Before very long, Roddy heard the drone of a motor car, far off in the woods. Reaching the road he chose a deeply shadowed covert under a pine from which to watch. Soon the drone of the car changed to a hum. Headlights gleamed intermittently through the trees. The car came on, passed by behind its bright yellow lights. And it was not a Ford. This afforded Roddy satisfaction, for that car surely had obliterated his tracks. He settled down to wait patiently. How long since he had been in the forest at night! The wilderness song in the treetops awakened dreamy memory of his hunting days in that country.

In half an hour or less he heard another automobile. At length the lights glimmered under the trees. This car slowed down before it reached him. When it passed, he recognized the Ford. The driver halted some few hundred feet from where Roddy sat. He or his companion got out with a flashlight and appeared to be scrutinizing the ground. Roddy grasped that they were looking for his tracks at the junction of the road to Wilcox. Muttering, impatient voices floated to Roddy. The waving light went out; a door clicked; the Ford moved on down the road out of sight.

Hurrying back through the woods Roddy was at some pains to locate his car. He found it, peered in the back to find Collie asleep. Then he got in, switched on the lights and cautiously drove back to the highway. Reaching it, he crossed to the left side and followed that down to the Wilcox branch on which he turned. Half a mile farther in the woods, he turned off on the rim road.

This was a forest road, seldom travelled by cars.

Grass and weeds grew as high as the running board; thick brush lined the sides, with an occasional black-trunked pine rising above. It led down into Jones' Canyon, at the bottom of which ran a creek difficult to ford in spring. But now there was only a dry wash. The slope up the ridge opposite, Roddy remembered, was steep and long. When he at last surmounted it to the ridge-top he felt relieved. All was smooth sailing now.

Collie called out something that sounded like where in the hell was he driving? Manifestly the slow grinding climb and severe jolts had roused her. Roddy told her to shut up and go to sleep. She exclaimed what a sweet boy he was turning out to joyride with, and then she subsided.

The forest road took a gradual ascent for twenty miles. Giant pines and silver spruce lined it so high that Roddy could not see their tips. It wound along the crest of the ridge, now through level areas of dense forest and then by heads of ravines that ran down into the canyons on each side. The woods smelled sweet with an odorous tang.

At length, some time late in the night, Roddy reached the Rim, where the road ran east and west. As the altitude was over eight thousand feet the air was bitingly cold. Roddy turned east. At times he passed close to the edge of the Rim where it broke abruptly into the great Tonto Basin. In the moonlight it showed its vast gulf, opaque and gray, reaching across to the black Matazels.

Driving became even more difficult owing to potholes, rocky places, sharp bends, hills and cross-washes. And often Roddy had to get out to drag aside rotten logs and branches that had recently toppled over. Therefore he had to advance slowly and carefully. The hours passed. He could keep account of his progress and whereabouts by the white signs along the road: Myrtle Creek, Barbershop Canyon, Quaking Asp, Leonard Canyon, Gentry Canyon, and at last Turkey Canyon.

Here he turned away from the Rim, straight down into the forest. The road had the same characteristics as the one by which he had reached the Rim, only now he was descending the winding crest of a ridge between the canyons. Toward the end, this road became well-nigh impassable, and full of rocks and gutters and boggy places. When he reached the end of the ridge, where it broke sharply down, the east was lightening and dawn was at hand.

Bright daylight greeted Roddy as he drove off the ridge into the beautiful park that was his objective. The old brown log cabin, with its mossy shelving roof, appeared as it existed in his memory, though even more weathered and picturesque than before. Here and there in the lonely park stood lofty pines and spruces; silver grass, colorful with autumn asters and daisies, covered the slopes; a wandering line of willow bushes, half-bronze, half-green, showed the course of the murmuring brook that flowed by the cabin; a grove of aspens, white-trunked and gold-leafed, blazed at the far end of the park.

Roddy's second glance caught the tawny gray coats of great antlered elk disappearing under the trees. He heard the gobble and cluck of wild turkeys. Down the brook two deer stood with long ears erect.

And all at once a strange feeling assailed Roddy, something stronger than the joy of solitude and beauty in the wilderness, a wish that he might have come there to stay.

Shutting off the engine he stepped out. The glistening frosted grass crackled under his feet. And at that moment Collie stuck her tousled bright head out of the car. She looked all around. When her eyes rested upon Roddy they were wide open, the sleep had vanished, and the topaz hue had darkened wondrously.

"*Lovely!*" she cried, rapturously. "Oh, what a paradise!" And she bounded out to hold up her red lips to him. "Mawning, Roddy. . . . You may—for bringing me heah."

Roddy did not kiss her, he did not want to, but he wondered at himself.

"You'll cuss me pronto," he replied, grimly.

"Never, darling. I feel like Alice in Wonderland." And she began to run around like a child who could not see all the enchanting things quickly enough.

Roddy unloaded the car of his camp duffle and food supplies. He split dead aspen and kindled a fire. Very shortly he had biscuits browning in a Dutch oven, coffeepot steaming, and he was slicing ham when Collie returned with her arms full of purple asters, goldenrod, and scarlet maple leaves. Her piquant face, smiling upon him from above this mass of exquisite color, gave him a distinct shock.

"Chuck that stuff and help me rustle breakfast," he said, surlily.

"Say, Mister, you won't go far with me on such talk as that," she retorted, her smile fading. She laid the flowers carefully aside and warmed her hands over the fire. Evidently they were numb. Then she got a bag out of the car and opened it upon the running board. Presently she went by with a towel and other toilet articles, to approach the brook. Suddenly a little shriek reached Roddy's ears. He laughed. She was a tenderfoot, even though she came from Texas. A few moments after that she came back, her face rosy and bright.

"Don't you supply your women with hot water?" she inquired, scornfully. "Or didn't they ever wash?" Then she returned to the car to brush her hair and apply her make-up, about which tasks she took her time.

"Come and get it before I throw it out," called Roddy.

She had a ravenous appetite, which might have been responsible for her unusual silence. "I'll say you can cook," she said presently, when she had finished. "I'll help you wash up."

Roddy did not reply. He was revolving in mind the need to tell her what he had done.

"You drove all night?"

"Yeah."

"You look tired—and cross. I'm afraid you're worried about those holdup men."

"Not any more. I gave them the slip."

"What place is this?"

"Turkey Canyon."

"That doesn't mean anything to me. But I saw turkeys. Oh, so tame and beautiful. Where are we?"

"Over a hundred miles from Hazelton. Half that from the road we drove down on."

"So far!" she exclaimed, wonderingly, but perplexed. "Why did you bring me heah?"

"I've kidnapped you," he replied, with a dark gaze at her.

"You—*what*?" Like a bent twig released she sprang up.

"I kidnapped you, Collie Younger."

"Honestly—you did?"

"Honest to God."

She sank to her knees in amazement. "Roddy! . . . Have my sins found me out?"

"I reckon they have."

"Oh!—I swear I didn't flirt with you. I was thrilled to death to meet a real Westerner, like some of the Texas riders my Dad used to tell me about. I—I liked you, Roddy Brecken. . . . And because—because . . . You took the chance to fool me—get me heah in this lonesome place. You fell for me!—" Incoherent though her amazement had made her, Collie's last words held a note of triumph which stung Roddy to immediate denial.

"Miss Younger, it may surprise you further to learn that I did not fall for you—at all," he rejoined with sarcasm.

Flaming red burned out the rouge in her cheeks.

"Then you kidnapped me for money?"

"I reckon so, partly."

"Who told you I had money?" And as he did not vouchsafe any answer to that she went on, her voice gaining in intensity. "Jack *told* you. I once showed him a letter from my brother about our oil wells in Texas. Jack must have told you."

"No. He never mentioned it."

"Then how did you know?"

"I didn't. You just jumped at conclusions."

"What do you mean by partly?"

"Well, as an after consideration, some dough is okay."

"I don't get you," she returned, shaking her curly head. "Cain't you come right out with it? *Why* did you kidnap me?"

"You made a sucker out of my brother," flashed Roddy, passionately.

"Oh—h!" she breathed softly, with a gasp of realization. "Yes, I did. I suppose the fact that the big conceited stiff deserved it will not get anywhere with you? . . . Well, heah we are. What do you think you're going to do with me?"

He regarded her brazenly, hiding in that bravado the conflict he was undergoing. He had not ever seen such a pair of tawny-fired eyes.

"You'll never play fast and loose with another guy."

"Do you intend to—to murder me?"

"I reckon I'll shy short of that."

"Then what?"

"You're curious, aren't you?"

"Why wouldn't I be curious? It seems to concern me."

"It'll concern you plenty before I get through with you. You'll be taught a lesson you'll never forget, you damn cheap little flirt. You'll think twice before you drive men crazy just to satisfy some female love of conquest. I'd think more of you if you'd gone the limit with every fellow you ever knew. Have you done that?"

"Why you—you backwoods lout!"

"All right. Call me what you like. The worse you cuss me the more kick I'll get out of handing you what *I* think you deserve."

"And what's that, Mr. Loyal Champion of Brother John?"

"Understand, Collie Younger," his voice rang out. "I don't care a damn for you. Last night you made one of your usual plays for me. It made me sore, instead of soft. All your prettiness, your white and gold skin, your curls, your come-hither eyes—don't mean one damn thing to me."

"Roddy Brecken, you *are* in love with me," she cried, triumphantly, and she held out her arms with a gesture, which, if it was as deceitful and vile as he believed, merited giving her all that rushed passionately to his mind.

"Yeah, you'll think so. You would!—When you slave for me, when I beat you, hog-tie you with a rope, make a rag out of you, till I trade what's left of you for money you're not worth!" So convincing did Roddy's fury make his words that Collie actually took them for truth.

"Jack will—kill you!" she whispered, ashen white under her rouge.

Roddy dropped his head. To look at her then was insupportable.

"For God's sake—Roddy—do *I* deserve that? . . . Oh, it's unthinkable. . . . Roddy, I swear I never did a dirty trick in my life—one that I *knew* was dirty."

"Well, begin now. Wash up these pans and pots. Use hot water and sand. Then pack your bags inside the cabin and clean it out. I'll go cut some bundles of spruce for beds."

The cold brutality of Roddy's response to her impassioned speech took all the fire out of Collie.

"Beds—in there?" she echoed, haltingly. "That buggy smelly place! I'd rather sleep outdoors."

"Well, if you prefer to freeze—but I don't—we'll both sleep inside."

"Roddy Brecken, if I sleep with you anywhere—I'll be cold plenty. I'll be daid!"

"Wait and see. You're a bluff, Collie Younger, and I'm calling you. Once in your life you're going to get the kicks you girls brag you like and never try. You'll show yellow."

"Much *you* know about girls. I won't do one single damn thing you order!"

"You won't, won't you?" rasped Roddy, and fastening a powerful hand in her blouse he jerked her off her feet and shook her until her curly head bobbed like a jumping-jack.

"You bum—You bully!" she choked out, furiously, when he let her go. And with all her might she slapped him. Roddy returned the blow in a heat that overcame him, and it was too violent for her slight weight and build. She went down limp as a sack. Rising on one hand, with the other at her red cheek, she glared up with eyes like molten bronze. A fierce animal pain possessed her. As it subsided she appeared prey to an incredulous awe. Roddy needed no more to see that not only had she never seriously felt pain, but she certainly had never received a blow until that moment.

"Rustle now, before I get mad," he ordered, and picking up his axe he stalked off toward the hillside. In all the fights Roddy had ever had, and they had numbered legion, he had never felt the fury this girl had aroused in him. On that score he tried to excuse himself for knocking her down. His threat to beat her had been merely threat. She was as imperious as the savage daughter of a great barbarian chief. She was also the epitome of the female species when infuriated, a cat, a spitfire. Lastly she was intelligent, keen as a whip. Roddy grasped that the one single advantage he had over her, the only thing he could resort to, was physical strength. By being a brute he could cow her. Chafing under this, he chopped down a small spruce tree and trimmed off the boughs. He gathered them into a huge bundle, and taking this up in his arms he staggered to the cabin and flung down the odorous mass under the projecting roof that had once covered a board porch.

He noted that Collie had packed all her baggage, and the bedding as well, to the cabin, and was now cleaning out the rubbish. He heard her sobbing before she came to the door with tears streaming down her cheeks. Roddy most decidedly did not undergo the satisfaction that such a sight should have given him. Instead, he felt like a cur. Whereupon he went back after another load of spruce, taking a long time about the task.

Upon returning he found that Collie had made a pretty good job of cleaning the cabin, had carried her bags in, and all of the spruce boughs and blankets. Peering in he saw her in the act of spreading the blankets over the branches. She had not ceased crying.

Roddy set to work packing his supplies in under

the porch roof, where he intended to build a fireplace of stones and cook the meals. While he was thus busied, Collie came to the door several times. Her expression seemed subdued.

"Stop your sniveling or I'll give you something to snivel about," he said, trying to make his voice as harsh as possible.

She did not reply, but the spirit flared up again in her eyes.

"Take that bag and fetch it back full of pinecones," he ordered brusquely.

After that he kept her at odd jobs until she appeared ready to drop. She was dirty and dishevelled. Her brown travelling suit was ruined. A discoloration began to be noticeable on her cheek. But all this did not deceive or placate Roddy. He knew that at any moment he must expect an earthquake or a volcanic eruption. All Collie needed was the spark. He advised her to go into the cabin and change to warmer clothes, outdoor garb and boots if she had them. He chopped a pile of firewood, and prepared lunch. When he called her there was no answer. He went into the cabin to find her lying on the blankets, pale and staring into space with tragic eyes.

"Roddy, I've been pondering," she said, without a trace of resentment in her voice, "You know women have a sixth sense. Intuition, clairvoyance, mysticism or whatnot. My faith in you has survived that brutal blow. I cain't explain it. There seems to be something wrong, unnatural, false in this situation. I don't get it. But despite what you've said and done—I don't believe you're rotten."

"Yeah? Well, come out and eat," he replied, in self-defense. He would be lost if he tried to bandy words with her or exchange intelligent thoughts or even argue. He feared she would see through him no matter how crude and hateful he could make himself. He was afraid of her in serious pondering mood. Collie followed him out without further words, but her look was enigmatic.

While Roddy ate, taciturn and silent, he brooded over how to follow up his advantage without sacrificing every vestige of self-respect. He hated her, he believed, yet . . . he did not finish the thought. He had to carry on. But an almost insuperable obstacle seemed to erect itself on the fact that, flirt though she might be, she was as game as she was pretty, and utterly in his power. This actuality made the pregnant difference.

3

THERE WAS A MOMENT THAT FOLLOWED, HOW SOON Roddy had no idea, in which he seemed to waver between what Collie had divined he really was and the character he had assumed. For her the situation, all at once raw and ominous, had brought out the graver, more womanly side of her. For Roddy that was harder to withstand than her provocative charms. He had to shock her out of it, kill it quickly, or fail utterly of his part in this impossible travesty. What of John's fatal attachment for this capricious girl, of the deal made and paid for?

With sombre eyes upon the appealing pale face, with gaze the passion of which was not pretense, though its reason was his own sick wrath at himself, Roddy deliberately crushed her intuitive faith in him, killed it with profane and coarse speech no man should ever have spoken to a woman. The horror she evinced, he knew, would soon merge into the loathing and fear he wanted her to feel. Then he stalked out of the cabin despising himself. There was little left, he thought bitterly, but to prove his infamous character in deeds.

Roddy took his rifle and went up the glade to hunt for turkeys. It was necessary to procure meat, although the hunting season was not yet open. Once on the wooded slope, however, he scarcely concentrated his faculties upon the pursuit of game. He sat down on a log to wipe his moist brow. The contending passions within his breast were not harmonious with the serenity, the beauty, the speaking solitude of this colorful forest. He could not sit still for long. He had to move, to walk, to climb. And he mounted the ridge that he had descended to get down to the park. He leaned against a huge fallen log, aware of the presence of a frisky red squirrel, the squall of a jay, of the flash of scarlet and orange and silver all around him. His consciousness of these sights and sounds was merely sensorial habit that he could not help. His thoughts and emotions were engaged in a grievous contention against what he knew not, except that it was not concerned with what he had promised to do for his brother. It was deeper than that. For minutes, perhaps hours, he paced the glades, the aisles under the pines, trying to bring to order the havoc in his mind. Then, all at once, he heard a hum foreign to the sounds of the wilderness. Lifting his head he seemed to suspend all his senses except hearing. The sound was not the drum of a grouse or the whirr of a turkey in flight. It was a motor, and the certainty again sharpened all his faculties. At first he thought the car was coming down the ridge from the Rim. But clearer perception proved it was ascending the hill. No car could have gone by, down into the park, without his hearing it.

"By heaven! Collie!" he cried. "She would—the game little Texan! And I never thought of it."

Roddy ran to intercept her, and he ran swiftly, leaping logs, crashing through brush, dodging trees. How far the road! He might be too late. The labor of the engine in low gear filled his beating ears. He rushed harder—burst out into the road.

Not a hundred feet down the grade the car came lurching and roaring up toward him. Roddy caught the gleam of Collie's face, the bright color of her hair.

"*Stop!*" he yelled, in stentorian voice, leaping to the middle of the road.

But she drove on, bumping to a short level, where the car gathered momentum. It bore down on Roddy. Collie leaned out to scream something indistinguishable. But her white face and piercing eyes needed no accompanying voice. She would run him down. Roddy had to leap to save his life.

Then in a swift dash he caught up with the car and bounded upon the running board. "Stop—damn you!" he panted.

"Jump—or I'll sideswipe you off!" she cried, resolutely.

Holding on, Roddy bent with groping hand for the ignition. He had a glimpse of her face, set and cold, her blazing gaze dead ahead.

"Jump! . . . *quick*!" she warned.

Roddy switched off the ignition. But the car kept rolling on a short downgrade.

"Brakes!—*Look out*!" yelled Roddy, frantically grasping the wheel. Collie had swerved toward the bank. He pulled. But she was strong and had a grip of steel. *Crash!* Flying glass stung Roddy as he was thrown off backward. He hit the ground hard. For an instant car and woods vanished in a scintillating burst of stars. Recovering, he sprang up. The car hung precariously over the bank, the front left wheel cramped against a tree.

"Collie!—Would—you—kill—us?" he panted, his chest lifting.

"I'd kill you damn gladly," she cut out, icily. Her eyes shone with an extraordinary sharpness.

"Come out of there," he yelled, seeing the car slip a little. Opening the door he seized her arm and jerked her out.

"You'll take it—right now—Texas!" he panted grimly, dragging her back to the road. He was vague about all he meant to do, but it included such a spanking as no girl ever got.

"I won't be man-handled, you dirty bum," she panted, struggling to free herself. But failing, she assailed him furiously, beating and scratching at his face, biting the arm that held her.

Then she kicked him violently on the shin. Her heavy-soled outing boot struck squarely on the bone, that, owing to an injury of long standing, had remained exquisitely sensitive. Roddy let out a yelp and, loosing her, sank down in agony. The forest reeled around him. Hard on that flamed up the fury of a savage. He saw the girl through red-filmed eyes. And utterly beside himself, as she kicked viciously at him again, he seized her leg and upset her. She screeched like a wild creature, and lying on her back kicked herself free. She sprang up but did not run. Roddy lurched erect to get his hands upon her. And when, after a moment of blind instinctive violence, he let go his hold, she sank limply on the ground, her face ashen, eyes glazed, with blood running from her lip.

"You Texas—wildcat!" he panted, gazing down with a sudden reversal to sanity. "Brought that—on yourself!"

He left her lying there in the middle of the pine-matted road. Out of breath, hot as fire, he limped over to the car. No serious damage had been done, but if it got started down the slope, and missed a couple of trees just wide enough to let it through, it would be a lost car. By rocking it he slipped the front left wheel off the tree. The right front wheel hung six inches above the grade. With stones blocking it up, Roddy thought he might back the car upon the road. He found one of Collie's suitcases on the seat, also a canteen of water and a coat wrapped around a parcel of food. These he removed to the ground, and cautiously getting in, he left the door open and started the engine. As he backed with full power on, the bank gave away and the car slid over. He lunged out just in the nick of time and, as luck would have it, fell on his bruised leg. Rising on one hand, mad with pain and the miserable circumstance, he watched the car go straight between the two trees and roll down into the brush out of sight, cracking and banging. Then there was a final heavy metallic crash on rocks.

"Ahuh! . . . That's that," muttered Roddy, and laboring to his feet he limped back up on the bank.

Collie lay where he had left her. As he approached he saw that her eyes were open, distended in dark horror.

"Oh—Roddy! . . . I heard it. . . . I—I thought you'd—gone over. . . ." she gasped, huskily. Fury in her, as in him, had evidently weakened at the imminence of death.

"You played hell—didn't you?" he queried, heavily.

"The car—smashed?"

"It pitched over the cliff."

"Then—we're stuck heah."

"Get up. You're not hurt."

She did not deny that in words, but observing her closely, as she dragged herself to her feet, he began to fear that he might have hurt her seriously. She could hardly stand erect, and her breathing seemed difficult.

"Can you walk?" he queried, conscious of shock.

"I'm all right. . . . After all—you're pretty big. . . . I'm only—a girl."

Roddy went mute at that. She was not accusing him but excusing herself for having been badly whipped in the fight with him. Was that the Texas of it? She had tried to sideswipe him off the running board, she had tried to kill him, she had fought him tooth and nail; and having lost she seemed to be as square as she was game. What a wonderful girl! Roddy saw her in an illuminating light.

"Come on," he said, proceeding to take up her bag and coat, and the canteen. Down the road some little distance he found his rifle. Thus encumbered, he could not help Collie. Slowly she followed him, a forlorn little figure now. Measured by his feelings, that descent to the cabin was indeed a long and grievous one for Roddy. If the girl had tried her feminine wiles, instead of pulling as nervy a stunt as he had ever heard of, he would have had no compunctions over continuing his program. But a change had begun to work in him, a change of opinion and heart. Still he had to keep up the deception until John came for them.

Arriving at the cabin, Roddy deposited his burdens and waited for Collie. It appeared to him that she would just about make it before collapsing. He had to subdue an impulse to go back and carry her. He judged correctly, for upon reaching the cabin, Collie fell upon the tarpaulin spread under the porch roof, and leaned back against the wall, spent and white.

"I've got to kill some meat," he said. "We can't

last here without meat. . . . I'll have to tie you up while I go hunting. If I'd done that . . ."

"I won't try to beat it again. . . . I couldn't, Roddy. Cain't you see when a girl is licked. Please don't tie me."

"I reckon I won't trust you."

"But you can. On my honor."

"On your what?"

Her spirit flared up faintly at that. "Of course *you* wouldn't."

Without more ado Roddy bound her ankles securely, cursing inwardly more because his hands shook so than at the heinous act he was performing. Then he slipped a packstrap tight round her waist and arms, and buckled it through the chinks between two logs at her back. All the while he avoided meeting her gaze. But even so the magnificent blaze of her eyes seemed to shrivel him.

"Roddy, you're a lot of things, the least of which is a damn fool," she said, enigmatically, as he picked up his rifle.

Stalking off he pondered her taunt. But upon reaching the woods at the end of the park he forcibly dismissed everything from mind except the important issue at hand, which was to procure meat. To that end, he stole into the aspens, on up the narrowing apex of the park, peering all around, and pausing every few paces to listen. He had not proceeded far when he heard turkeys scratching. This was a difficult sound to locate. Apparently it was above him. The afternoon wind was strong from the north. He worked against that. He heard various other noises. Once he stopped short with abated breath at a distant burr that he took for a motorcar. He waited long for a repetition. As it did not come he concluded he had been mistaken. Nerves! He would always be hearing the hum of a car in the forest.

Roddy located the flock of turkeys busily and noisily engaged in scratching for pine nuts. The wind was right from them to him, and he kept out of sight while making the stalk. Creeping close he shot two gobblers before the flock disintegrated in a flapping, thumping escape. Much gratified at his success Roddy tied the legs of the turkeys together, threw them over his shoulder, and picking up his rifle made down the slope for camp. Straightway then his problem with Collie reasserted itself, perceptibly different again and more vexatious.

When he strode out from under the pines, at the foot of the north slope, he saw Collie leaning against the cabin wall where he had tied her. As he approached, Roddy imagined her face even paler. Her eyes resembled black holes in a white blanket. She had watched for his return. Poor kid! Roddy's conscience flayed him. Right there he felt forming in him the nucleus of a revolt against John's preposterous plot.

He crossed the brook. He was within speaking distance and was about to hail Collie when something about her checked the words behind his lips. Her unnatural rigidity, her blanched face—no! it was a strained and lightning flash of eyes.

Roddy hurried on. What was wrong with Collie? Even as he interpreted that magic of her eyes as deliberate, a warning of impending peril, a harsh voice rasped out:

"Drop that rifle! Stick 'em up!"

Roddy obeyed. A man ran out of the cabin at Roddy. A thin red beard failed to hide his hard lips and narrow chin. He held an automatic gun levelled before him. A second fellow appeared, gun in one hand, rope in the other.

"Frisk him, Marty," ordered the foremost. In short order Roddy's big roll of bills, his knife and watch, his wallet were tossed upon the grass. The cold gray eyes of the leader snapped as he saw them. Then, in short order Roddy was bound hand and foot, and shoved like a sack of meal to the ground. His head bumped against one of his supply packs.

"Collie?" he burst out, as soon as he could speak.

"Okay. They had just got heah. Cain't you use your eyes? A Texas ranger would have been wise the instant he caught my look."

"Ah!—I saw—I thought . . . but I'm no Texas ranger," rejoined Roddy, heavily.

The man called Marty was a Westerner, unmistakably, but a ragged lout whose sallow visage Roddy had seen on the corners or in the poolrooms of Hazelton. He picked up his gun, which he had laid aside to bind Roddy, and shoving it back into his hip pocket he turned to his accomplice. Roddy recognized in this individual the man who had attempted to hold him up on the road the day before. He was under thirty. The singularly cold and fanatic expression of his pasty face proclaimed him an addict to drugs. He was counting the many bills in Roddy's roll.

"How much, Gyp?" queried Marty, his bleary eyes rolling eagerly.

"Over two grand. But that's not a patch of what we'll clean up. Marty, you steered me on to something good." Then he turned to Roddy, his scrutiny intense and penetrating.

"John Brecken's brother, eh?"

"Yes."

"Yeah, and John Brecken's best girl," leered the fellow Marty.

"And all tied up tight. That means that she didn't come willing," cogitated the red-bearded one, putting two and two together. "Kidnapped her, eh?" he asked, turning to Roddy.

Roddy made no reply.

"Oh, you won't answer. Well, you don't have to. It's as plain as the nose on your face. If you stole John Brecken's girl, he'll pay to get her back and he'll pay to get you back just so he can get even with you. Now, ain't that a sweet dish?"

"Yeah," chimed in Marty, "and John Brecken's rich. Owns a store, a garage and an interest in the sawmill. He ought to come acrost plenty, Gyp."

"Who's the dame? Does she have any folks that would be happy to have their little tootsie-wootsie safe home again?" inquired Gyp.

"She doesn't live in Hazelton. College girl. Never heard her name."

Gyp approached Collie, to get down on one knee before her.

"What's your name, sweetness?"

"I guess it's Dennis."

"Say! You're all bunged up besides being tied. Beat you up, did he!"

"No. I tried to escape. Ran the car over a bank."

"I see. That's why we couldn't find the car we tracked down here. . . . Have your folks got any money?"

"My mother works to send me to college."

"Don't try to kid me, sweetheart. Could you get ten thousand dollars for ransom?"

"John Brecken ought to pay that much for me," replied Collie, sarcastically.

The gangster arose with a light upon his pale visage.

"Plenty safe, Marty, I'll say. Lovely hideout to wait, good eats when we were damn near starved, a pretty little dame to sleep with—a swell layout! Lemme dope this out while you cook supper. My mouth's watering for turkey."

"I'm shore a no-good cook," replied the lout, too heartily to doubt.

"Little one, you're on the spot," said Gyp, to Collie.

"I'm afraid I cain't stand on my feet," she replied.

"Hey, girl snatcher, can you roast a turkey so it'll melt in my mouth?" called the fellow to Roddy.

"I reckon. But hardly while my hands and feet are tied."

"Untie him, Marty. And stand guard over him with a gun while he gets supper."

The instant Roddy was freed and on his feet he began to think of a way to turn the tables on their captors. There would still be several hours of daylight. He must work slowly, watching like a hawk, thinking with all the wit and cunning he could muster. Marty fetched the turkeys to him and Roddy began to pick off the feathers. Gyp went back to Collie. Roddy saw him sit down to lay a bold hand on her. Then, Roddy, with the blood turning to fire in his veins, dared not look again. But he could hear the man talking low, manifestly making love to Collie. While Roddy heard, he thought desperately. How much more than Collie's life had he to save now! That transformed his sombre spirit. He recalled then that his gun was in the side pocket of the car. But his rifle lay only a few paces away in the grass under some bushes. Apparently his captors had forgotten that. As a last resort, even with Marty sitting there, weapon in hand, Roddy decided he would leap for the rifle. But before being driven to that he must wait and watch for a safer moment.

"You dirty skunk. Take your hands off me!" suddenly cried Collie, her voice rising to a shriek. It had such withering abhorrence that Roddy marveled how any man could face, let alone touch, any woman who spoke with such passion. The fellow on guard let out a lecherous guffaw. Roddy, acting on a powerful impulse, edged over to kindle a fire. On his knees he split wood to replenish it.

"Need hot fire—so it'll burn down—bed of coals," he explained, huskily. But he put his big skillet on the blazing fagots and poured half a can of grease into it, then added a quart of water. He had conceived a cunning though exceedingly dangerous plan.

When Collie broke into hysterical sobs the gangster got up. "Say, baby," he said, caustically, "if I wasn't hard up for a dame, I'd call you a washout. You cut that stuff or I'll give you something to squawk about."

Then he took to walking to and fro, apparently in deep thought. Roddy was fearful that he might come across the rifle. But he paced a beat between the cabin and the campfire. His concentration became so great that he forgot the others. No doubt he was working out details of the plot to extort ransom money from John Brecken. That plot no longer concerned Roddy. It would never even get started into action.

Roddy put on the Dutch oven to heat. The greasy water in the skillet had begun to boil. Roddy watched it, listened to it simmer. The last of the water in his bucket he poured into a pan with flour. It was not enough to mix biscuit dough. But he fussed with other utensils and supplies until the grease and water in the skillet threatened to boil over.

The moment had come. Strong and cool, with his passion well under control, Roddy had two arrows to his bow.

"Can I fetch a bucket of water?" he asked.

"No. Stay there," called Gyp, coming to the fire. "Marty, you get it."

Marty took the bucket and slouched toward the brook.

Gyp looked down upon the fire. "Say, it strikes me you're slow."

"Slow—but sure," replied Roddy, bending to grasp the skillet.

With an incredibly swift movement he came up with it to fling the scalding contents squarely into Gyp's face. The fellow let out a hideous scream of agony.

Roddy sprang to snatch up his rifle. Wheeling as he cocked it, he saw the blinded man fire from his pocket. Roddy shot him through the heart, and his awful curses ended in a gulp. He was swaying backward when Roddy whirled to look for the other fellow. At that instant he heard a bucket clang on rock and a yell. Marty emerged from the willows with his gun spouting red. Roddy felt something like wind, then a concussion that rocked him to his knees. A white flash burst into a thousand sparks before his sight. But as it cleared he got a bead on Marty and pulled the trigger.

The fellow bawled with the terror of a man shot through the middle. His arms spread out wide. The gun in his right hand smoked and banged. Roddy, quick as a flash, worked the lever and bored the man again.

Blank-visaged and slack, he swayed back to crash through the willows that lined the brook.

Then Roddy, blinded by his own blood, dropped the rifle and bent over, one hand supporting him, the other pulling out his handkerchief. Hot blood poured down his face. He heard it drip on the grass. As fast as he wiped it off it streamed down again.

Collie was calling: "Roddy! . . . *Roddy!* . . . Oh, my God—the blood!"

"I'm shot, Collie, but . . . where are you?"

"Heah!—heah! . . . *heah*!"

He crawled on hands and knees, guided by her voice.

"Wipe off—the blood."

"I cain't—I cain't! Darling, I'm tied!"

"Can you see where I'm shot?"

"Yes. Your head—on top—all bloody . . . but Roddy it can't be bad. You've got your senses."

"I feel as if my brains were oozing out."

"Mercy!—No! No! That cain't be, Roddy . . . cut these ropes."

Roddy felt in his pockets. "They took my knife," he said, and then blindly he began to unbuckle the strap that held her elbows to her sides. It seemed to take long. He reeled dizzily. An icy sickening nausea assailed him.

"There! Let me get at that rope round my feet. . . . Damn, you would tie such a knot!"

He felt her bounce up and heard her swift feet thudding away and back to him. A towel went over his head and face. Ministering hands pressed it down.

"Oh, the blood pours so fast! I cain't see," she cried. "I'll feel." And with shaking fingers she felt for the wound. Then Roddy sank under a pain that might have been a red-hot poker searing his bared brain. Collie was crying into his fading consciousness. "Darling! Only a groove! No hole in your skull. Oh, thank God!" then Roddy lost all sense.

When he came to, his blurred sight seemed to see trees and slopes through a red film. His first clear thought was of the blood that had trickled over his eyes. A splitting pain burned under his skull. But his weak hand felt a dry forehead and then a damp bandage bound round his scalp. The red hue, then, he grasped, was sunset flooding the park.

"Collie," he called, faintly.

She came pattering out of the cabin to thump to her knees. Topaz eyes with glinting softness searched his face. "Roddy!"

"I'm okay—I guess."

"Oh, boy! You came to twice, out of your haid."

"Yeah? Well, I can get it now. My head hurts awful. But I can remember—and think. . . . Collie, I reckon I did for those two hombres."

"You sure did. That Gyp dog is lying right heah by the fire, daid as a door-nail, and the other is down by the creek. . . . I screamed like a Comanche when you threw that skillet of scalding water in his eyes. I watched him then. . . . I never batted an eyelash. . . . Saw you kill him!—But when the other one shot you and you went down—Oh, God, that was terrible. I lost my nerve. And never got it back till you fainted."

"Collie, nerve is your middle name. You're one grand kid. Can you ever forgive me? Oh, you couldn't! I'm a sap to ask."

"Yes, I forgive you. Maybe I deserved it. If only I could get all this straight!—But heah, let's talk of our predicament. . . . Your wound is not serious. I washed it out with Mercurochrome. Lucky I had some in my bag. No fear of infection. I can keep your fever down with this brook water, which is ice-cold. But you've lost blood—Oh, so much! That frightened me. You cain't walk for a long time. Our car is smashed. Of course those men hid theirs, but maybe we can find it. I wouldn't mind staying heah forever. It's so sweet and wild and lovely. I'm a Texas girl, Roddy, you'd find that I can cook and chop wood and shoot game—dress it, too. That'd be swell. But, oh, I'm so worried. You might need a doctor."

"Collie, everything will be all right," replied Roddy, with thought only to relieve her. "Jack will come after us in ten days."

"Heah?"

"Aw!—You see—I . . ." Roddy had betrayed himself and could not retrieve his blunder. He bit his lip. The girl's face flashed scarlet, then went as white as a sheet. And her eyes transfixed him.

"Roddy, you framed me."

He groaned in his abasement and try as he might he could not stand those accusing eyes.

"Why in the world—*why*?" she cried, poignantly. Then evidently she saw that his physical strength was not equal to his distress. "Never mind, Roddy. Forget it. That's not our immediate problem. There's plenty of work for little Collie, believe me. Now I'll make good my brag."

For moments Roddy lay with closed eyes on the verge of fading away again. But the acute pain held him to sensibility. He heard Collie bustling about the campfire. She roused him presently to give him a hot drink. Dusk had fallen. The red light left the sky. He could not keep his eyes open. Collie covered him with blankets. He felt her making a bed beside him. Then all went black.

In the night he awoke, burning, throbbing, parched with thirst. Collie heard his restless movements. She rose to minister to him. She had placed a bucket of water at hand. She gave him a drink and bathed his face. The air was piercingly cold. Coyotes were howling off in the darkness. While Collie was tucking the blankets around him, Roddy fell asleep. Later he awoke again, but endured his pain and did not arouse her. The pangs, however, could not keep him awake long.

The daylight came, Roddy did not know when.

There was ice on the water in the bucket, but he did not feel cold. All day he suffered. All day Collie stayed near to keep a wet towel on his face. He craved only water to drink. That night he slept better. Next morning the excruciating headache had gone. His wound throbbed, but less and less. He was on the mend.

That day Collie half carried, half dragged him into the cabin to the bough bed under the window. She made a bed for herself on the ground close by. She was in and out all day long.

When she had made Roddy comfortable, she brought him his package of money. "Took this out of Gyp's pocket," she explained briefly, with an involuntary shudder.

Roddy thanked her in a weak voice. It was an effort to talk, but his mind grew active once more. He had no appetite, but forced down what food and drink she brought him. As he slowly recovered, it grew harder for him to face her. There must come a reckoning. He divined it; and her care, her kindness, her efficiency added to his shame. Night was a relief.

Next day he struggled to his feet, and walked out, wavering, light-headed, weak as an infant. He noted that Collie had covered the bodies of the dead men with large piles of brush and tarpaulins. In another day or two, Roddy thought, he would be strong enough to bury them. Even now the buzzards were circling around high overhead.

While the warm sun was melting the hoarfrost on grass and leaves, Roddy walked and rested and walked again, slowly regaining his strength. All about him were signs that Collie's vaunted efficiency at camp tasks was no vain boast. The campfire had been moved under the end of the porch where Collie had built up a rude fireplace with stones. She had even strung up a clothesline on which several intimate garments were fluttering with an air of domesticity, and was busy now carrying buckets of water up from the creek. And this was the girl he thought would make such a poor wife for John!

That third day Collie had little to say to Roddy until late in the afternoon, when, as he lay on his bed in the cabin, with the gold sunlight flooding in at the window, she entered with an armful of purple asters.

"My favorite wildflowers, Roddy."

"Mine too. . . . Isn't it funny that we have one thing in common?"

"I could tell you more."

"Yeah."

She knelt beside his bed and leaned close to him. "Roddy, you're doing fine. You'll be well soon. I'm so glad. We can have some walks—maybe a hunt—before . . . Tell me now, darling."

Roddy protested and denied and demurred, but in the end, from his procrastination, his lies, his evasions, she pieced together the whole cloth of this miserable travesty.

"You great big sap! . . . Roddy, did you ever read the story of Miles Standish, who got John Alden to do his wooing for him? Don't you remember when Priscilla said: 'Why don't you speak for yourself, John?' "

"Never was much of a reader," replied Roddy, evasively. His chest seemed to cave in.

She leaned over him with soft look and touch and tone. "That day at Canyon Creek, when I went in swimming in only my brassiere and panties to torment Jack—you fell in love with me didn't you?"

"No! I—I thought you a little brazen hussy."

"Sure, I was. But that's not the point. You fell for me, didn't you?"

"I did not."

"Roddy! . . . Then at the dance, when I asked you to hold me close?"

"Collie, you're a fiend. You're all—almost all, Jack . . . No, I didn't fall for you then."

"When you kidnapped me?"

"Nor then, either."

"Big Boy, it took you long, didn't it?" she laughed, adorably, "Well, then, when you caught me running away in the car—and I kicked you—*heah*—on your shin?" And she laid a tender hand on his leg, to move it gently, caressingly, he imagined in his bewilderment, over the great bruise.

"Collie, don't you kid me," he implored.

"When you beat me half daid—was it *then*, darling?"

"Collie, you win, callous little flirt that you are!" he burst out, hoarsely. "It must have been at the creek, when you pulled your shameless stunt—and all those other times. But, honest to God, I never knew it till that dirty Gyp laid hands on you!"

"It doesn't make any difference *when*, so long as you *do*, Roddy," she said, more softly, leaning her face so close that he began to tremble. Could not the insatiate little creature be satisfied without flaying her victim? "Say you love me!"

"I reckon."

"More than Jack did?"

"Yes."

"More than any boy ever loved me?" she ended, imperiously.

"God help me, Collie, I'm afraid I do," he replied, huskily. "Now I'm punished. I'll take my medicine. But don't rub it in. This has been a rotten deal for you. It's proved you to be one grand little thoroughbred. It'll help me, too, I hope, to make a man out of myself. And when you . . ."

She was bending to him, her heavy eyelids

closed, her expression rapt and dreamy, her sweet lips curved and tremulous with the kiss she meant to bestow, when Roddy saw her start. He eyes opened wide, dark, flashing, luminous with inquiry.

"Listen," she whispered. "A car!"

"By gosh!—You're right. It's coming down the ridge. A forest ranger—or hunter . . . Oh, Collie, it means deliverance for you."

"No, Roddy," she cried, a note of triumph in her voice, "I've got a hunch it's your brother Jack, showing yellow, jealous, scared, come to square himself with us."

"Jack?" questioned Roddy in astonishment.

From the window they watched the leafy gateway of the road at the foot of the ridge. Collie put a tense arm round Roddy. He felt that if Jack really confronted him there, the world would either come to an end or suddenly be glorious.

A bright car slid out of the foliage

"Jack and his new car! Look at him, sneaking along so slowly!" cried Collie, gleefully, and giving Roddy a squeeze she rolled off the bed. To Roddy's amazement she disarranged her blouse, rumpled her curls, vehemently rubbed the make-up from her face, all in a flash. "Will I hand it to him? I'm telling you, darling . . . Lie down. Pretend to be dying. Let *me* do the talking." She moved to the wide opening of the cabin, and assumed a tragic pose.

The front of the shining car showed beyond the corner of the wall. It stopped. The click of door and thud of feet brought their visitor to the cabin.

"Collie!—*Collie!*" It was Jack's voice, betraying a decided panic.

"So!—You're heah ahaid of schedule?—But too late, Jack Brecken!"

"Too late? What do you mean? Collie, what's happened?" he exclaimed fearfully.

"Happened! What usually happens when a man carries a girl off into the woods alone?" Collie's tone held all the drama of a wronged woman.

For a moment Jack was speechless. "Why—Collie—" he stammered then, "you don't mean that—that Roddy—"

"He's only human, Jack."

"But—Oh, hell! I didn't dream he'd—Roddy did that?" For a moment his tone was utterly incredulous. Then fury possessed him and he burst out, "The dirty dog—Where is he?"

Roddy listened, spellbound, half in horror, half in admiration. What an actress she was.

"After all, you can't blame him," retorted Collie accusingly. "This was your scheme. I should think you wouldn't have dared. Roddy loved you, Jack, and that was why he fell for your crazy idea."

Her stinging words had the effect of quelling Jack's rage.

"Collie," he said, and his voice filled with anguish, "after you left, I realized what I had done. That's why I came to confess, to make amends, I—"

"Too late, Jack," cut in Collie, in solemn accents. "You brother lies in heah—his head shot open!"

In the silence that ensued, Roddy heard John's gasping explosion of breath.

"God almighty! *You killed him!*" John's knees shook so that they were incapable of holding him. He sat down on the pile of canvas behind him.

Collie started. For a moment she could not find words and the pause must have been a lifetime of hell to the stricken man. Then she stuck her head in the door to wink a glowing eye at Roddy.

"Jack Brecken, now that you've realized what could have happened, I'll tell you the truth," she pealed out, her slim form instilled with a liberation of passion. "Roddy is not daid. He's alive—and I love him—love him—love him—love him. . . . Your plot miscarried, you big sap! Roddy kidnapped me all right, but we both were kidnapped by real kidnappers. They planned to make you pay ransom. Oh, that would have been great! But one of them got fresh with me and would have attacked me. Roddy outwitted him—killed him—and his partner. Jack, I was on the fence about you. I think I would have married you. Thank heaven, I found you out, and at last fell terribly in love with your wicked kidnapping brother."

Relief struggled with anguish in John's pale face. "Roddy—not—dead?" he gasped, "and—and—he—killed two men—?" Then looking fearfully around, "Where are they?"

Collie's tone was extremely casual. "One of them is over by the creek," she drawled, "and you're sitting on the other."

OUTLAWS OF PALOUSE

·1·

THE LONE HORSEMAN RODE SLOWLY UP THE SLOPE, bending far down from his saddle in the posture customary for a range rider when studying hoof tracks. The intensity of his scrutiny indicated far more than the depth or direction of these imprints in the dust.

Presently the rider sat up and turned in his saddle to look back. While pondering the situation his eagle eyes swept the far country below. It was a scene like hundreds of others limned upon his memory—a vast and rugged section of the West, differing only in the elements of color, beauty, distance and grandeur that characterized the green Salmon River Valley, the gray rolling range beyond, the dead-white plain of alkali and the purple sawtoothed peaks piercing the sky in the far distance.

That the tracks of the stolen Watrous thoroughbreds would lead over the range into Montana had been the trailer's foregone conclusion. But that the mysterious horse thieves had so far taken little care to conceal their tracks seemed a proof of how brazen this gang had become. On the other hand Dale Brittenham reflected that he was a wild-horse hunter—that a trail invisible to most men would be like print to him.

He gazed back down the long slope into Idaho, pondering his task, slowly realizing that he had let himself in for a serious and perhaps deadly job.

It had taken Dale five hours to ride up to the point where he now straddled his horse, and the last from which he could see the valley. From here the stage road led north over the divide into the wild timbered range.

The time was about noon of an early summer day. The air at that height had a cool sweet tang, redolent of the green pines and the flowered mountain meadows. Dale strongly felt the beauty and allurement of the scene, and likewise a presentiment of trouble. The little mining town of Salmon, in the heyday of its biggest gold producing year—1886—nestled in a bed of the shining white and green river. Brittenham had many enemies down there and but few friends. The lonely life of a wild-horse hunter had not kept him from conflict with men. Whose toes might he not step upon if he tracked down those horse thieves? The country was infested with road agents, bandits, horse thieves; and the wildest era Idaho had ever known was in full swing.

"I've long had a hunch," Dale soliloquized broodingly. "There're men down there, maybe as rich and respectable as Watrous himself, who're in cahoots with these thieves. . . . Cause if there wasn't, this slick stealin' couldn't be done."

The valley shone green and gold and purple under the bright sun, a vast winding range of farms, ranches, pastures, leading up to the stark Sawtooth Mountains, out of which the river glistened like a silver thread. It wound down between grassy hills to meander into the valley. Dale's gaze fastened upon an irregular green spot and a white house surrounded by wide sweeping pastures. This was the Watrous ranch. Dale watched it, conscious of a pang in his heart. The only friendship for a man and love of a woman he had ever known had come to him there. Leale Hildrith, the partner of Jim Watrous in an extensive horse-breeding and trading business, had once been a friend in need to Brittenham. But for Hildrith, the wild-horse hunter would long before have taken the trail of the thieves who regularly several times a year plundered the ranches of the valley. Watrous had lost hundreds of horses.

"Dale, lay off," Hildrith had advised impatiently. "It's no mix of yours. It'll lead into more gunplay, and you've already got a bad name for that. Besides, there's no telling where such a trail might wind up."

Brittenham had been influenced by the friend to whom he owed his life. Yet despite his loyalty, he wondered at Hildrith's attitude. It must surely be that Hildrith again wanted to save him from harm, and Dale warmed to the thought. But when, on this morning, he had discovered that five of Edith Watrous's thoroughbreds, the favorite horses she loved so dearly, had been stolen, he said no word to anyone at the ranch and set out upon the trail.

At length Brittenham turned his back upon the valley and rode on up the slope toward the timberline, now close at hand. He reached the straggling firs at a point where two trails branched off the road. The right one led along the edge of the timberline and on it the sharp tracks of the shod horses showed plainly in the dust.

At this junction Dale dismounted to study the tracks. After a careful scrutiny he made the deduction that he was probably two hours behind the horse thieves, who were plainly lagging along. Dale found an empty whiskey bottle, which was still damp and strong with the fumes of liquor. This might in some measure account for the carelessness of the thieves.

Dale rode on, staying close to the fir trees, between them and the trail, while he kept a keen eye ahead. On the way up he had made a number of conjectures, which he now discarded. This branching off the road puzzled him. It meant probably that the horse thieves had a secret rendezvous somewhere off in this direction. After perhaps an hour of travel along the timber belt Dale entered a rocky region where progress was slow, and he came abruptly upon a wide, well-defined trail running at right angles to the one he was on. Hundreds of horses had passed along there, but none recently. Dale got off to reconnoiter. He had stumbled upon something that he had never heard the riders mention—a trail which wound up the mountain slope over an exceedingly rough route. Dale followed it until he had an appreciation of what a hard climb, partly on foot, riders must put themselves to, coming up from the valley. He realized that here was the outlet for horse thieves operating on the Salmon and Snake River ranges of Idaho. It did not take Dale long to discover that it was a one-way trail. No hoof tracks pointing down!

"Well, here's a rummy deal!" he ejaculated. And he remembered the horse traders who often drove bands of Montana horses down into Idaho and sold them all the way to Twin Falls and Boise.

Those droves of horses came down the stage road. Suddenly Dale arrived at an exciting conclusion. "By thunder! Those Montana horses are stolen, too. By the same gang—a big gang of slick horse thieves. They steal way down on the Montana ranges—drive up over a hidden trail like this to some secret place where they meet part of their outfit who've been stealin' in Idaho. . . . Then they switch herds. . . . And they drive down, sellin' the Montana horses in Idaho and the Idaho horses in Montana. . . . Well! The head of that outfit has got brains. Too many to steal Jim Watrous's fine blooded stock! That must have been a slip. . . . But any rider would want to steal Edith Watrous's horses!"

Returning to his mount, Dale led him in among the firs and rocks, keeping to the line of the new trail but not directly upon it. A couple of slow miles brought him to the divide. Beyond that the land sloped gently, the rocks and ridges merged into a fine open forest. His view was unobstructed for several hundred yards. Bands of deer bounded away from in front of Dale to halt and watch with the long ears erect. Dale had not hunted far over that range. He knew the Sawtooth Mountains in as far as Thunder Mountain. His wild-horse activities had been confined to the desert and low country toward the Snake River. Therefore he had no idea where this trail would lead him. Somewhere over this divide, on the eastern slope, lived a band of Palouse Indians. Dale knew some of them and had hunted wild horses with them. He had befriended one of their number, Nalook, to the extent of saving him from a jail sentence. From that time Nalook had been utterly devoted to Dale, and had rendered him every possible service.

By midafternoon Brittenham was far down on the forested tableland. He meant to stick to the trail as long as there was light enough to see. His saddlebag contained meat, biscuits, dried fruit and salt. His wild-horse hunts often kept him weeks on the trail, so his present pursuit presented no obstacles. Nevertheless, as he progressed he grew more and more wary. He expected to see a log cabin in some secluded spot. At length he came to a brook that ran down from a jumble of low bluffs and followed the trail. The water coursed in the alternate eddies and swift runs. Beaver dams locked it up into little lakes. Dale found beaver cutting aspens in broad daylight, which attested to the wildness of the region. Far ahead he saw rocky crags and rough gray ridgetops. This level open forest would not last much further.

Suddenly Brittenham's horse shot up his ears and halted in his tracks. A shrill neigh came faintly to the rider's ears. He peered ahead through the pines, his nerves tingling.

But Dale could not make out any color or movement, and the sound was not repeated. This fact somewhat allayed his fears. After a sharp survey of his surroundings Dale led his horse into a clump of small firs and haltered him there. Then, rifle in hand, he crept forward from tree to tree. This procedure was slow work, as he exercised great caution.

The sun sank behind the fringe of timber on the high ground and soon shadows appeared in thick parts of the forest. Suddenly the ring of an ax sent the blood back to Dale's heart. He crouched down behind a pine and rested a moment, his thoughts whirling. There were campers ahead, or a cabin; and Dale strongly inclined to the conviction that the horse thieves had halted for the night. If so, it meant they were either far from their rendezvous or taking their time waiting for comrades to join them. Dale pondered the situation. He must be decisive, quick, ruthless. But he could not determine what to do until he saw the outfit and the lay of the land.

Wherefore he got up, and after a long scrutiny ahead he slipped from behind the tree and stole on to another. He repeated this move. Brush and clumps of fir and big pines obstructed any considerable survey ahead. Finally he came to less thick covering on the ground. He smelled smoke. He heard faint indistinguishable sounds. Then a pinpoint of fire gleamed through the thicket in front of him. Without more ado Dale dropped on all fours and crawled straight for that light. When he got to the brush and peered through, his heart gave a great leap at the sight of Edith Watrous's horses staked out on a grassy spot.

Then he crouched on his knees, holding the Winchester tight, trying to determine a course of action. Various plans flashed through his mind. The one he decided to be the least risky was to wait until the thieves were asleep and quietly make away with the horses. These thoroughbreds knew him well. He could release them without undue excitement. With half a night's start he would be far on the way back to the ranch before the thieves discovered their loss. The weakness of this plan lay in the possibility of a new outfit joining this band. That, however, would not deter Dale from making the attempt to get the horses.

It occurred to him presently to steal up on the camp under cover of the darkness and if possible get close enough to see and hear the robbers. Dale lay debating this course and at last yielded to the temptation. Dusk settled down. The nighthawks wheeled and uttered their guttural cries overhead. He waited patiently. When it grew dark he crawled around the thicket and stood up. A bright campfire blazed in the distance. Dark forms moved to and fro across the light. Off to the left of Dale's position there appeared to be more cover. He sheered off that way, lost sight of the campfire, threaded a careful approach among trees and brush, and after a long detour came up behind the camp, scarcely a hundred yards distant. A big pine tree dominated an open space lighted by the campfire. Dale selected objects to use for cover and again sank to his hands and knees. Well he knew that the keenest of men were easier to crawl up on than wild horses at rest. He was like an Indian. He made no more noise than a snake. At intervals he peered above the grass and low brush. He heard voices and now and then the sputtering of the fire. He rested again. His next stop would be behind a windfall that now obscured the camp. Drawing a deep breath, he crawled on silently without looking up. The grass was wet with dew.

A log barred Dale's advance. He relaxed and lay quiet, straining his ears.

"I tell you, Ben, this hyar was a damn fool job," spoke up a husky-voiced individual. "Alec agrees with me."

"Wal, I shore do," corroborated another man. "We was drunk."

"Not me. I never was more clear-headed in my life," replied the third thief, called Ben. His reply ended with a hard chuckle.

"Wal, if you was, no one noticed it," returned Alec sourly. "I reckon you roped us into a mess."

"Aw hell! Big Bill will yelp with joy."

"Mebbe. Shore he's been growin' overbold these days. Makin' too much money. Stands too well in Halsey an' Bannock, an' Salmon. Cocksure no one will ever find our hole-up."

"Bah! Thet wouldn't faze Big Bill Mason. He'd bluff it through."

"Aha! Like Henry Plummer, eh? The coldest proposition of a robber thet ever turned a trick. Had a hundred men in his outfit. Stole damn near a million in gold. High respected citizen of Montana. Mayor of Alder Gulch. . . . All the same he put his neck in the noose!"

"Alec is right, Ben," spoke up the third member in his husky voice. "Big Bill is growin' wild. Too careless. Spends too much time in town. Gambles. Drinks. . . . Someday some foxy cowboy or hoss hunter will trail him. An' that'll be about due when Watrous finds his blooded horses gone."

"Wal, what worries me more is how Hildrith will take this deal of yours," said Alec. "Like as not he'll murder us."

Brittenham sustained a terrible shock. It was like a physical rip of his flesh. Hildrith! These horse thieves spoke familarly of his beloved friend. Dale grew suddenly sick. Did not this explain Leale's impatient opposition to the trailing of horse thieves?

"Ben, you can gamble Hildrith will be wild," went on Alec. "He's got sense if Big Bill hasn't. He's Watrous's pardner, mind you. Why, Jim Watrous would hang him."

"We heerd talk this time that Hildrith was goin' to marry old Jim's lass. What a hell of a pickle Leale will be in!"

"Fellers, he'll be all the stronger if he does grab thet hoss-lovin' gurl. But I don't believe he'll be so lucky. I seen Edith Watrous in town with thet cowboy Les Crocker. She shore makes a feller draw his breath hard. She's young an' she likes the cowboys."

"Wal, what of thet? If Jim wants her to marry his pardner, she'll have to."

"Mebbe she's a chip off the old block. Anyway, I've knowed a heap of women an' thet's my hunch. . . . Hildrith will be as sore as a bunged-up thumb. But what can he do? We got the hosses."

"So, we have. Five white elephants! Ben, you've let your cravin' for fine hoss-flesh carry you away."

An interval of silence ensued, during which Dale raised himself to peer guardedly over the log. Two of the thieves sat with hard red faces in the glare of the blaze. The third had his back to Dale.

"What ails *me*, now I got 'em, is can I keep 'em," this man replied. "Thet black is the finest hoss I ever seen."

"They're all grand hosses. An' thet's all the good it'll do you," retorted the leaner of the other two.

"Ben, them thoroughbreds air known from Deadwood to Walla Walla. They can't be sold or rid. An' shore as Gawd made little apples, the stealin' of them will bust Big Bill's gang."

"Aw, you're a couple of yellow pups," rejoined Ben contemptuously. "If I'd known you was goin' to show like this I'd split with you an' done the job myself."

"Uhuh! I recollect now thet *you* did the watchin' while Steve an' me stole the horses. An' I sort of recollect dim-like thet you talked big about money while you was feedin' us red likker."

"Yep, I did—an' I had to get you drunk. Haw! Haw!"

"On purpose? Made us trick the outfit an' switch to your job?"

"Yes, on purpose."

"So! . . . How you like this on purpose, Ben?"

hissed Alec, and swift as a flash he whipped out a gun. Ben's hoarse yell of protest died in his throat with the bang of the big Colt.

The bullet went clear through the man to strike the log uncomfortably near Dale. He ducked instinctively, then sank down again, tense and cold.

"My Gawd! Alec, you bored him," burst out the man Steve.

"I shore did. The damn bullhead! . . . An' thet's our out with Hildrith. We're gonna need one. I reckon Big Bill won't hold it hard agin us."

Dale found himself divided between conflicting courses—one, to shoot these horse thieves in their tracks, and a stronger one, to stick to his first plan and avoid unnecessary hazard. Wherewith he noiselessly turned and began to crawl away from the log. He had to worm under spreading branches. Despite his care, a dead limb, invisible until too late, caught on his long spur, which gave forth a ringing metallic peal. At the sudden sound, Dale sank prone, his blood congealing in his veins.

"Alec! You hear thet?" called Steve, his husky voice vibrantly sharp.

"By Gawd I did! . . . Ring of a spur! I know thet sound."

"Behind the log!"

The thud of quick footsteps urged Dale out of his frozen inaction. He began to crawl for the brush.

"There Steve! I hear someone crawlin'. Smoke up thet black patch!"

Gunshots boomed. Bullets thudded all around Dale. Then one tore through his sombrero, leaving a hot sensation in his scalp. A gust of passion intercepted Dale's desire to escape. He whirled to his knees. Both men were outlined distinctly in the firelight. The foremost stood just behind the log, his gun spouting red. The other crouched peering into the darkness. Dale shot them both. The leader fell hard over the log, and lodged there, his boots beating a rustling tattoo on the ground. The other flung his gun high and dropped as if his legs had been chopped from under him.

Brittenham leaped erect, working the lever of his rifle, his nerves strung like wires. But the engagement had ended as quickly as it had begun. He strode into the campfire circle of light. The thief Ben lay on his back, arms wide, his dark visage distorted and ghastly. Dale's impulse was to search these men, but resisting it he hurriedly made for the horses. The cold sick grip on his vitals eased with hurried action, and likewise the fury.

Presently he reached the grassy plot where the horses were staked out. They snorted and thumped the ground.

"Prince," he called, and whistled.

The great stallion whinnied recognition. Dale made his way to the horse. Prince was blacker than the night. Dale laid gentle hands on him and talked to him. The other horses quieted down.

"Jim . . . Jade . . . Ringspot . . . Bluegrass," called Dale, and repeated the names as he passed among the horses. They were all pets except Jade, and she was temperamental. She had to be now. Presently Dale untied her long stake rope, and after that the ropes of the other horses. He felt sure Prince and Jim would follow him anywhere, but he did not want to risk it then.

He led the five horses back, as nearly as he could, on the course by which he had approached the camp. In the darkness the task was not easy. He chose to avoid the trail, which ran somewhere to his left. A tree and a thicket here and there he recognized. But he was off his direction when his own horse nickered to put him right again.

"No more of that, Hoofs," he said, when he found his animal. Cinching his saddle, he gathered up the five halters and mounted. "Back trail yourself, old boy!"

The Watrous horses were eager to follow, but the five of them abreast on uneven and obstructed ground held Dale to a slow and watchful progress. Meanwhile, as he picked his way, he began figuring the situation. It was imperative that he travel all night. There seemed hardly a doubt that the three thieves would be joined by others of their gang. Anyone save a novice could track six horses through a forest. Dale meant to be a long way on his back trail before dawn. The night was dark. He must keep close to the path of the horse thieves so that he would not get lost in this forest. Once out on the stage road he could make up for slow travel.

Trusting to Hoofs, the rider advanced, peering keenly into the gloom. He experienced no difficulty in leading the thoroughbreds; indeed they often slacked their halters and trampled almost at his heels. They knew they were homeward bound, in the charge of a friend. Dale hoped all was well, yet could not rid himself of a contrary presentiment. The reference of one of the horse thieves to Ben's doublecrossing their comrades seemed to Dale to signify that the remaining outfit might be down in the Salmon River Valley.

At intervals Dale swerved to the left far enough to see the trail in the gloom. When he could hear the babble of the brook he knew he was going right. In due time he worked out of the open forest and struck the grade, and eventually got into the rocks. Here he had to follow the path, but he endeavored to keep his tracks out of it. And in this way he found himself at length in a shallow, narrow gulch, the sides of which appeared unscalable. If it were short, all would be well; on the other hand he distrusted a long defile, where it would be perilous if he happened to encounter any riders. They would scarcely be honest riders.

The gulch was long. Moreover it narrowed and was dark as pitch except under the low walls. Dale did not like Hoof's halting. His trusty mount had the nose and the ears of the wild horses he had hunted for years.

"What ails you, hoss?" queried Dale.

Finally Hoofs stopped. Dale, feeling for his ears, found them erect and stiff. Hoofs smelled or heard something. It might be a bear or a cougar, both of which the horse disliked exceedingly. It might be more horse thieves, too. Dale listened and thought hard. Of all things, he did not want to retrace his steps. While he had time then, and before he knew what menaced further progress, he dismounted and led the horses as far under the dark wall as he could get them. Then he drew their heads up close to him and called low, "Steady, Prince. . . . Jade, keep still. . . . Blue, hold now. . . ."

Hoofs stood at his elbow. It was Dale's voice and hand that governed the intelligent animals. Then as a low trampling roar swept down the gully they stood stiff. Dale tingled. Horses coming at a forced trot! They were being driven when they were tired. The sound swelled, and soon it was pierced by the sharp calls of riders.

"By thunder!" muttered Dale, aghast at the volume of sounds. "My hunch was right! . . . Big Bill Mason has raided the valley. . . . Must be over a hundred head in that drove!"

The thudding, padded roar, occasionally emphasized by an iron-shod hoof ringing on stone, or a rider's call, swept down the gully. It was upon Dale before he realized the drove was so close. He could see a moving, obscure mass coming. He smelled dust. "Git in thar!" shouted a weary voice. Then followed a soft thudding of hoofs on sand. Dale's situation was precarious, for if one of his horses betrayed his whereabouts, there would be a rider sheering out for strays. He held the halters with his left hand, and pulled his rifle from its saddle sheath. If any of these riders bore down on him, he would be forced to shoot and take to flight. But his thoroughbreds, all except Jade, stood like statues. She champed her bit restlessly. Then she snorted. Dale hissed at her. The moment was one to make him taut. He peered through the gloom, expecting riders to loom up, and he had the grim thought that it would be death for them. Then followed a long moment of sustained suspense, charged with incalculable chance.

"Go along there, you lazy hawses," called a voice.

The soft thumping of many hoofs passed. Voices trailed back. Dale relaxed in immeasurable relief. The driving thieves had gone by. He thought then for the first time what a thrilling thing it was going to be to return these thoroughbreds to Edith Watrous.

Hard upon that came the thought of Leale Hildrith—his friend. It was agony to think that Leale was involved with these horse thieves. On the instant Dale was shot through with the memory of his debt to Hildrith—of that terrible day when Hildrith had found him out on the range, crippled, half starved and frozen, and had, at the risk of his own life, carried Dale through the blizzard to the safety of a distant shelter. A friendship had sprung up between the two men, generous and careless on Hildrith's part, even at times protective. In Dale had been engendered a passionate loyalty and gratitude, almost a hero worship for the golden-bearded Hildrith.

What would come of it all? No solution presented itself to Dale at the moment. He must meet situations as they arose, and seek in every way to protect his friend.

Toward sunset the following day Dale Brittenham rode across the clattering old bridge, leading the Watrous thoroughbreds into the one and only street of Salmon. The dusty horses, five abreast, trotting at the end of long halters, would have excited interest in any Western town. But for some reason that puzzled Dale, he might have been leading a circus or a band of painted Indians.

Before he had proceeded far, however, he grasped that something unusual accounted for the atmosphere of the thronged street. Seldom did Salmon, except on a Saturday night, show so much activity. Knots of men, evidently in earnest colloquy, turned dark faces in Dale's direction; gaudily dressed dancehall girls, black-frocked gamblers, and dusty-booted, bearded miners crowded out in the street to see Dale approach; cowboys threw up their sombreros and let out their cracking whoops; and a throng of excited youngsters fell in behind Dale, to follow him.

Dale began to regret having chosen to ride through town, instead of fording the river below and circling to the Watrous ranch. He did not like the intense curiosity manifested by a good many spectators. Their gestures and words, as he rode by, he interpreted as more speculative and wondering than glad at his return with the five finest horses in Idaho.

When Dale was about halfway down the wide street, a good friend of his detached himself from a group and stepped out.

"Say, Wesley, what'n hell's all this hubbub about?" queried Brittenham as he stopped.

"Howdy, Dale," returned the other, offering his hand. His keen eyes flashed like sunlight on blue metal and a huge smile wrinkled his bronzed visage. "Well, if I ain't glad to see you I'll eat my shirt. . . . Just like you, Dale, to burst into town with thet bunch of hosses!"

"Sure, I reckoned I'd like it. But I'm gettin' leery. What's up?"

"Hoss thieves raided the river ranches yesterday," replied the other swiftly. "Two hundred head gone! . . . Chamberlain, Trash, Miller—all lost heavy. An' Jim Watrous got cleaned out. You know, lately Jim's gone in for cattle buyin', an' his riders were away somewhere. Jim lost over a hundred head. He's ory-eyed. An' they say Miss Edith was heartbroke to lose hers. Dale, you sure got the best of her other beaux with this job."

"Stuff!" ejaculated Dale, feeling the hot blood in his cheeks, and he sat up stiffly. "Wes, damn you—"

"Dale, I've had you figgered as a shy hombre with girls. Every fellow in this valley, except you, has cocked his eyes at Edith Watrous. She's a flirt, we all know. . . . Listen. I been achin' to tell you my sister Sue is a friend of Edith an' she says Edith likes you pretty well. Hildrith only has the inside track cause of her father. I'm tellin' you, Dale."

"Shut up, Wes. You always hated Hildrith, an' you're wrong about Edith."

"Aw, hell! You're scared of her an' you overrate what Hildrith did for you once. Thet's all. This was the time for me to give you a hunch. I won't shoot off my chin again."

"An' the town's all het-up over the horse-thief raid?"

"You bet it is. Common talk runs thet there's some slick hombre here who's in with the hoss thieves. This Salmon Valley has lost nigh on to a thousand head in three years. An' every one of the big raids comes at a time when the thieves had to be tipped off."

"All big horse-thief gangs work that way," replied Dale, ponderingly. Wesley was trying to tell him that suspicion had fallen upon his head. He dropped his eyes as he inquired about his friend Leale Hildrith.

"Humph! In town yesterday, roarin' louder than anybody about the raid. Swore this stealin' had to be stopped. Talked of offerin' ten thousand dollars reward—that he'd sent an outfit of riders after the thieves. You know how Leale raves. He's in town this morning, too."

"So long, Wes," said Dale soberly and was about to ride on when a commotion broke the ring of bystanders to admit Leale Hildrith.

Dale was not surprised to see the golden-bearded, booted-and-spurred partner of Watrous, but he did feel a surprise at a fleeting and vanishing look in Hildrith's steel-blue eyes. It was a flash of hot murderous amazement at Dale there with Edith Watrous's thoroughbreds. Dale understood it perfectly, but betrayed no sign.

"Dale! You son-of-a-gun!" burst out Hildrith in boisterous gladness, as he leaped to seize Dale's hand and pumped it violently. His apparent warmth left Dale cold, and bitterly sad for his friend. "Fetched Edith's favorites back! How on earth did you do it, Dale? She'll sure reward you handsomely. And Jim will throw a fit. . . . Where and how did you get back these horses?"

"They were stolen out of the pasture yesterday mornin' about daylight," replied Dale curtly. "I trailed the thieves. Found their camp last night. Three men, callin' themselves Ben, Alec an' Steve. They were fightin' among themselves. Ben tricked them, the other two said. An' one of them shot him. . . . They caught me listenin' an' forced me to kill them."

"You killed them!" queried Hildrith hoarsely, his face turning pale. His eyes held a peculiar oscillating question.

"Yes. An' I didn't feel over-bad about it, Leale," rejoined Dale with sarcasm. "Then I wrangled the horses an' rode down."

"Where—was this?"

"Up on the mountain, over in Montana somewhere. After nightfall I sure got lost. But I hit the stage road. . . . I'll be movin' along, Leale."

"I'll come right out to the ranch," replied Hildrith, and hurried through the crowd.

"Open up there," called Dale to the staring crowd. "Let me through."

As he parted the circle and left it behind, a taunting voice cut the silence. "Cute of you, Dale, fetchin' the high-steppers back. Haw! Haw!"

Dale rode on as if he had not heard, though he could have shot the owner of that mocking voice. He had been implicated in this horse stealing. Salmon was full of shifty-eyed, hardlipped men who would have had trouble in proving honest occupations. Dale had clashed with some of them, and he was hated and feared. He rode on through town and out into the country. He put the horses to a brisk trot, as he wanted to reach the Watrous ranch ahead of Hildrith.

Dale stood appalled at the dual character of the man to whom he considered himself so deeply indebted, whom he had looked on as a friend and loved so much. It was almost impossible to believe. Almost every man in the valley liked Leale Hildrith and called him friend. The women loved him, and Dale felt sure, despite Wesley's blunt talk, that Edith Watrous was one of them. And if she did love him, she was on the way to disgrace and misery. Leale, the gay handsome blade, not yet thirty, so good-natured and kindly, big-hearted and openhanded, was secretly nothing but a low-down horse thief. Dale had hoped against hope that when he saw Hildrith the disclosures of the three horse thieves would somehow be disproved. But that had not happened. Hildrith's eyes, in only a flash, had betrayed him. Dale suffered the degradation of his own disillusion. Yet the thought of Edith's unhappiness hurt him even more.

He had not gotten anywhere in his perplexed and bewildered state of mind when the bronze-and-gold hills of the Watrous ranch loomed before him. From the day he had ridden up to it, Dale had loved this great ranch, with its big old weatherbeaten house nestling among the trees up from the river, its smooth shining hills bare to the gray rocks and timberline, its huge fields of corn and alfalfa green as emerald, its level range spreading away from the river gateway to the mountains. From that very day, too, Dale had loved the lithe, free-stepping, roguish-eyed daughter of Jim Watrous—a melancholy and disturbing fact that he strove to banish from his consciousness. Her teasing and tormenting, her fits of cold indifference and her resentment that she could not make him bend to her like other admirers, her flirting before his eyes plainly to make him jealous—all these weaknesses of Edith's did not equal in sum her kindness to him, and the strange inexplicable fact that when she was in trouble she always came to him.

As Dale rode around the grove into the green square where the gray ranch house stood on its slope, he was glad to see that Hildrith had not arrived. Three saddled horses standing bridles down told Dale that Watrous had callers. They were on the porch and they had sighted him. Crowding to the high steps, they could be heard exclaiming. Then gray-haired Jim Watrous, stalwart of build and ruddy of face, descended down a step to call lustily, "Edith! Rustle out there. Quick!"

Dale halted on the green below the porch. It was going to be a hard moment. Watrous and his visitors could not disturb him. But Edith! . . . Dale heard the swift patter of light feet—then a little scream, sweet, high-pitched, that raised a turbulent commotion in his breast.

"Oh Dad! . . . My horses!" she cried in ecstasy, and she clasped her hands.

"They sure are, lass," replied Watrous gruffly.

"Ha! Queer Brittenham should fetch them," added a man back of Watrous.

In two leaps Edith came down the high steps, supple as a cat, and bounded at Dale, her bright hair flying, her dark eyes shining.

"Dale! Dale!" she cried rapturously, and ran to clasp both hands around his arm. "You wild-horse hunter! You darling!"

"Well, I'll stand for the first," said Dale, smiling down at her.

"You'll stand for that—and hugs—kisses when I get you alone, Dale Brittenham. . . . You've brought back my horses! My heart was broken. I was crazy. I couldn't eat or sleep. . . . Oh, it's too good to be true! Oh, Dale, I can never thank you enough."

She left him to throw her arms around Prince's dusty neck and to cry over him. Watrous came slowly down the steps, followed by his three visitors, two of whom Dale knew by sight. He bent the eyes of a hawk upon Dale.

"Howdy, Brittenham. What have you got to say for yourself?"

"Horses talk, Mr. Watrous, same as money," replied Dale coolly. He sensed the old horse trader's doubt and dismay.

"They sure do, young man. There's ten thousand dollars' worth of horseflesh. To Edith they're priceless. What's your story?"

Dale told him briefly, omitting the description of the horse-thief trail and the meeting upon it with the raided stock from the valley. He chose to save these details until he had had more time to ponder over them.

"Brittenham, can you prove those three horse thieves are dead—an' that you made away with two of them?" queried Watrous tensely.

"Prove!" ejaculated Dale, sorely nettled. "I could prove it—certainly, sir, unless their pards came along to pack them away. . . . But my word should be proof enough, Mr. Watrous."

"I reckon it would be, for me, Brittenham," returned the rancher hastily. "But this whole deal has a queer look. . . . This gang of horse thieves has an accomplice—maybe more than one—right here in Salmon."

"Mr. Watrous, I had the same thought," said Dale shortly.

"Last night, Brittenham, your name was whispered around in this connection."

"That doesn't surprise me. Salmon is full of crooked men. I've clashed with some. I've only a few friends an'—"

Edith whirled to confront her father with pale face and blazing eyes.

"Dad! Did I hear aright? What did you say?"

"I'm sorry, lass. I told Brittenham he was suspected of bein' the go-between for this horse-thief gang."

"For shame, father! It's a lie. Dale Brittenham

would not steal, let alone be a cowardly informer."

"Edith, I didn't say I believed it," rejoined Watrous, plainly upset. "But it's bein' said about town. It'll fly over the range. An' I thought Brittenham should know."

"You're right, Mr. Watrous," said Dale. "Thank you for tellin' me."

The girl turned to Dale, evidently striving for composure.

"Come, Dale. Let us take the horses out."

She led them across the green toward the lane. Dale had no choice but to follow, though he desperately wanted to flee. Before the men were out of range of his acute hearing, one of them exclaimed to Watrous, "Jim, he didn't deny it!"

"Huh! Did you see his eyes?" returned the rancher shortly. "I'd not want to be in the boots of the man who accuses him to his face."

"Here comes Hildrith, drivin' as if the devil was after him." Dale heard the clattering buckboard, but he did not look. Neither did Edith. She walked with her head down, deep in thought. Dale dared to watch her, conscious of inexplicable feelings.

The stable boy, Joe, ran out to meet them, with a face that was a study in inexpressible wonder and delight. Edith did not relinquish the halters until she had led the horses up the incline into the wide barn.

"Joe, water them first," she said. "Then wash and rub them down. Take a look at their hoofs. Feed them grain and a little alfalfa. And watch them every minute till the boys get back."

"Yes, Miss Edith, I shore will," he replied eagerly. "We done had word they'll be hyar by dark."

Dale dismounted and removed saddle and bridle from his tired horse.

"Let Joe watch your horse, Dale. I want to talk to you."

Dale leaned against some bales of hay, not wholly from weariness. He had often been alone with Edith Watrous, but never like this.

"Reckon I ought to—to clean up," he stammered, removing his sombrero. "I—I must look a mess."

"You're grimy and worn, yes. But you look pretty proven and good to me, Dale Brittenham. . . . What's that hole in your hat?"

"By thunder! I forgot about that. It's a bullet hole."

"Oh—so close . . . Who shot it there, Dale?"

"One of the horse thieves."

"It was self-defense, then?"

"You bet it was."

"I've hated your shooting scrapes, Dale," she rejoined earnestly. "But here I see I'm squeamish—and unreasonable. . . . Only the reputation you have—your readiness to shoot—that's all I never liked about it."

"I'm sorry. But I can't help that," replied Dale, turning his sombrero round and round with restless hands.

"You needn't be sorry this time. . . . Dale, look me straight in the eye."

Thus so earnestly urged, Dale had to comply. Edith appeared pale of face and laboring under suppressed emotion. Her dark eyes had held many expressions for him, mostly roguish and coquettish, and sometimes blazing, but at this moment they were beautiful with a light, a depth he had never seen in them before. And it challenged him with a truth he had always driven from his consciousness—that he loved this bright-haired girl.

"Dale, I was ashamed of Dad," she said. "I detest that John Stafford. He is the one who brought the gossip from town—that you were implicated in this raid. I don't believe it."

"Thanks, Edith. It's good of you."

"Why didn't you say something?" she asked spiritedly. "You should have cussed Dad roundly."

"I was sort of flabbergasted."

"Dale, if this whole range believed you were a horse thief, I wouldn't. Even if your faithful Nalook believed it—though he never would."

"No. I reckon that Indian wouldn't believe bad of me."

"Nalook thinks heaps of you, Dale—and—and that's one reason why I do—too."

"Heaps?"

"Yes, heaps."

"I'd never have suspected it."

"Evidently you never did. But it's true. And despite your—your rudeness—your avoidance of me, now is the time to tell it."

Dale dropped his eyes again, sorely perturbed and fearful that he might betray himself. Edith was not bent on conquest now. She appeared roused to championship of him, and there was something strange and soft about her that was new and bewildering.

"I never was rude," he denied stoutly.

"We won't argue about that now," she went on hurriedly. "Never mind about me and my petty vanity. . . . I'm worried about this gossip. It's serious, Dale. You'll get into trouble and go gunning for somebody—unless I keep you from it. I'm going to try. . . . Will you take a job riding for me—taking care of my horses?"

"Edith! . . . I'm sure obliged to you, for that offer. But Watrous wouldn't see it."

"I'll make him see it."

"Hildrith? . . . He wouldn't like that idea—now."

"Leale will like anything I want him to."

"Not this time."

"Dale, *will* you ride for me?" she queried impatiently.

"I'd like to—if—if . . . Well, I'll consider it."

"If you would that'd stop this gossip more than anything I can think of. . . . I'd like it very much, Dale. I'll never feel safe about my horses again. Not until these thieves are rounded up. If you worked for me I could keep you here—out of that rotten Salmon. And you wouldn't be going on those long wild-horse hunts."

"Edith, you're most amazin' kind an'—an' thoughtful all of a sudden." Dale could not quite keep a little bitter surprise out of his voice.

She blushed vividly. "I might have been all that long ago if you had let me," she replied.

"Who am I to aspire to your kindness?" he said almost coldly. "But even if I wasn't a poor wild-horse hunter I'd never run after you like these—these—"

"Maybe that's one reason why . . . well, never mind," she interrupted, with a hint of her old roguishness. "Dale, I'm terribly grateful to you for bringing back my horses. I know you won't take money. I'm afraid you'll refuse the job I offered. . . . So, Mister Wild-Horse Hunter, I'm going to pay you as I said I would—back at the house."

"No!" he cried, suddenly weak. "Edith, you wouldn't be so silly—so— Aw, it's just the devil in you."

"I'm going to, Dale."

Her voice drew him as well as her intent; and forced to look up, he was paralyzed to see her bending to him, her face aglow, her eyes alight. Her hands flashed upon his shoulders—slipped back—and suddenly pressed like bands of steel.

Dale somehow recovered strength to stand up and break her hold.

"Edith, you're out of—your head," he said huskily.

"I don't care if I am. I always wanted to, Dale Brittenham. This was a good excuse. . . . And I'll never get another."

The girl's face was scarlet as she drew back from Dale, but it paled before she concluded her strange speech.

"You're playin' with me—you darned flirt," he blurted out.

"Not this time, Dale," she replied soberly, and then Dale grasped that something deeper and hitherto unguessed had followed hard on her real desire to reward him for his service.

"It'll be now or never, Dale . . . for this morning at breakfast I gave in at last to Dad's nagging—and consented to marry Leale Hildrith."

"Then it'll be never, my strange girl," replied Dale hoarsely, shot through with anguish for Edith and his treacherous friend. "I—I reckoned this was the case. . . . You love Leale?"

"I think—I do," replied Edith, somewhat hesitantly. "He's handsome and gay. Everybody loves Leale. You do. All the girls are mad about him. I—I love him, I guess. . . . But it's mostly Dad. He hasn't given me any peace for a year. He's set on Hildrith. Then he thinks I ought to settle down—that I flirt—that I have all his riders at odds with each other on my account. . . . Oh, it made me furious."

"Edith, I hope you will be happy."

"A lot *you* care, Dale Brittenham."

"I cared too much. That was the trouble."

"*Dale!* . . . So that was why you avoided me?"

"Yes, that was why, Edith."

"But you are as good as any man."

"You're a rich rancher's daughter. I'm a poor wild-horse hunter."

"Oh! As if that made any difference between friends."

"Edith, it does," he replied sadly. "An' now they're accusin' me of bein' a horse thief. . . . I'll have to kill again."

"No! You musn't fight," she cried wildly. "You might be shot. . . . Dale, promise me you'll not go gunning for anyone."

"That's easy, Edith. I promise."

"Thanks, Dale. . . . Oh, I don't know what's come over me." She dropped her head on his shoulder. "I'm glad you told me. It hurts but it helps somehow. I—I must think."

"You should think that you must not be seen—like this," he said gently.

"I don't care," she flashed, suddenly aroused. Edith's propensity to change was one of her bewildering charms. Dale realized he had said the wrong thing and he shook in her tightening grasp. "You've cheated me, Dale, of a real friendship. And I'm going to punish you. I'm going to keep my word, no matter what comes of it. . . . Oh, you'll believe me a flirt—like Dad and all of those old fools that think I've kissed these beaux of mine. But I haven't, well, not since I was a kid. Not even Leale! . . . Dale, you might have kissed me if you'd had any sense."

"Edith, have you lost all sense—of—of—" he choked out.

"Of modesty? . . . I'm not in the least ashamed." But her face flamed as she tightened her arms around him and pressed sweet cool lips to his cheek. Dale was almost unable to resist crushing her in his arms. He tried, weakly, to put her back. But she was strong, and evidently in the grip of some emotion she had not calculated upon. For her lips sought his and their coolness turned to sweet fire. Her eyelids fell heavily. Dale awoke to spend his hunger for love and his renunciation in passionate response.

That broke the spell which had moved Edith.

"Oh, Dale!" she whispered, as she wrenched her lips free. "I shouldn't have. . . . Forgive me. . . . I was beside myself."

Her arms were sliding from his neck when quick footfalls and the ring of spurs sounded in the doorway. Dale looked up to see Hildrith, livid under his golden beard, with eyes flaring, halting at the threshold.

"What the hell!" he burst out incredulously.

Dale's first sensation was one of blank dismay, and as Edith, with arms dropping, drew back, crimson of face, he sank against the pile of bales like a guilty man caught in some unexplainable act.

"Edith! What did I see?" demanded Hildrith in jealous wrath.

"Not very much! You were too late. Why do you slip up on people like that?" the girl returned with a tantalizing laugh. She faced him, her blush and confusion vanishing. His strident voice no doubt roused her imperious spirit.

"You had your arms around Dale?"

"I'm afraid I had."

"You kissed him?"

"Once. . . . No, twice, counting a little one," returned this amazing creature. Dale suffered some kind of torture only part of which was shame.

"Well, by heaven!" shouted Hildrith furiously. "I'll beat him half to death for that."

Edith intercepted him and got between him and Dale. She pushed him back with no little force.

"Don't be a fool, Leale. It'd be dangerous to strike Dale. Listen. . . ."

"I'll call him out," shouted her lover.

"And get shot for your pains. Dale has killed half a dozen men. . . . Let me explain."

"You can't explain a thing like this."

"Yes, I can. I admit it looks bad, but it really isn't. . . . When Dale brought my horses back, I was so crazy with joy that I wanted to hug and kiss him. I told him so. But I couldn't before Dad and all those men. When we came out here I—tried to, but Dale repulsed me."

"Edith, do you expect me to believe that?" interposed Hildrith.

"Yes, it's true. . . . But the second time I succeeded—and you almost caught me in the act."

"You damned little flirt!"

"Leale, I wasn't flirting. I wanted to kiss Dale; I was in rapture about my horses. And before that Dad and those men hinted Dale was hand and glove with these horse thieves. I hated that. It excited me. Perhaps I was out of my head. Dale said I was. But you shall not blame him. It was my fault."

"Oh hell!" fumed Hildrith in despair. "Do you deny the poor beggar is in love with you?"

"I certainly do deny that," she retorted, and her gold-tan cheeks flamed red.

"Well, he is. Anybody could see that."

"I didn't. And if it's true he never told me."

Hildrith began to pace the barn. "Good God! Engaged to marry me for half a day, and you do a brazen thing like that. . . . Watrous is sure right. You need to be tied down. Playing fast and loose with every rider on the range! Coaxing your Dad to set our marriage day three months off! . . . Oh, you drive me mad. I'll tell you, young woman, when you *are* my wife . . ."

"Don't insult me, Mr. Hildrith," interrupted Edith coldly. "I'm not your wife yet. . . . I was honest with you, because I felt sure you'd understand. I'm sorry I told you the truth and I don't care whether you believe me or not."

With her bright head erect, she walked past Hildrith, avoiding him as he reached for her, and she was deaf to his entreaties.

"Edith, I'll take it all back," he cried after her. But so far as Dale could see or hear she made no response. Hildrith turned away from the door, wringing his hands. It was plain that he worshipped the girl, that he did not trust her, that he was inordinately suspicious, that for an accepted lover he appeared the most wretched of men. Dale watched him, seeing him more clearly in the revelation of his dual nature. Just how far Hildrith had gone with this horse-stealing gang, Dale did not want to know. Dale did see that his friend's redemption was possible—that if he could marry this girl, and if he could be terribly frightened with possible exposure, he might be weaned from whatever association he had with Mason, and go honest and make Edith happy. It was not a stable conviction, but it gripped Dale. He had his debt to pay to Hildrith and a glimmering of a possible way to do it formed in his mind. Even at that moment, though, he felt the ax of disillusion and reality at the roots of his love for this man. Hildrith was not what he had believed him. But that would not deter Dale from paying his debt a thousandfold. Lastly, if Edith Watrous loved this man, Dale felt that he must save him.

Hildrith whirled upon Dale. "So this is how you appreciate what I've done for you, Dale. You made love to my girl. You damned handsome ragamuffin—you worked on Edith's sympathy! You've got me into a hell of a fix."

"Leale, you sure are in a hell of a fix," replied Dale with dark significance.

"What do you mean?" queried Hildrith sharply, with a quick uplift of head.

"You're one of Big Bill Mason's gang," rejoined Dale deliberately.

Hildrith gave a spasmodic start, as if a blade had pierced his side. His jaw dropped and his face blanched to an ashen hue under his blond beard. He tried to speak, but no words came.

"I sneaked up on the camp of those three horse thieves. I listened. Those low-down thieves—Ben, Alec, Steve—spoke familiarly of you. Alec an' Steve were concerned over what you'd do about the theft of the Watrous horses. Ben made light of it. He didn't care. They talked about Big Bill. An' that talk betrayed you to me. . . . Leale, you're the range scout for Mason. You're the man who sets the time for these big horse raids."

"You know. . . . Oh, my God!" cried Hildrith abjectly.

"Yes, I know that an' more. I know the trail to Mason's secret rendezvous. I was on that trail an' saw this last big drove of stolen horses pass by. I figured out how Mason's gang operates. Pretty foxy, I'll say. But it was too good, too easy, too profitable. It couldn't last."

"For God's sake, Dale, don't squeal on me!" besought Hildrith, bending over Dale with haggard, clammy face. "I've money. I'll pay you well—anything. . . ."

"Shut up! Don't try to buy me off, or I'll despise you for a yellow cur. . . . I didn't say I'd squeal on you. But I do say you're a madman to think you can work long at such a low-down game."

"Dale, I swear to God this was my last deal. Mason forced me to one more, a big raid which was to be his last in this valley. He had a hold on me.

We were partners in a cattle business over in Montana. He roped me into a rustling deal before I knew what it actually was. That was three years ago, over in Kalispell. Then he found a hiding place—a box canyon known only to the Indians—and that gave him the idea of raiding both Montana and Idaho ranges at the same time—driving to the canyon and there changing outfits and stolen horses. While a raid was on over there, Mason made sure to be in Bannock or Kalispell, and he roared louder than anyone at the horse thieves. He had the confidence of all the ranchers over there. My job was the same here in the Salmon Valley. But I fell in love with Edith and have been trying to break away."

"Leale, you say you swear to God this was your last deal with Mason?"

"Yes, I swear it. I have been scared to death. I got to thinking it was too good to last. I'd be found out. Then I'd lose Edith."

"Man, you'd not only lose her. But you'd be shot—or worse, you'd be hanged. These ranchers are roused. Watrous is ory-eyed, so Wesley told me. They'll organize an' send a bunch of Wyomin' cowboys out on Mason's trail. I'll bet that's exactly what Watrous is talkin' over now with these visitors."

"Then it's too late. They'll find me out. God! Why didn't I have some sense?"

"They won't find you out if you quit. Absolutely quit! I'm the only man outside the Mason gang who knows. If some of them are captured an' try to implicate you, it wouldn't be believed. I'll not give you away."

"Dale, by heaven, that's good of you," said Hildrith hoarsely. "I did you an injustice. Forgive me. . . . Dale, tell me what to do. I'm in your hands. I'll do anything. Only save me. I wasn't cut out for a horse thief. It's galled me. I've been sick after every raid. I haven't the guts. I've learned an awful lesson."

"Have you any idea how Edith would despise you, if she knew?"

"That's what makes me sweat blood. I worship the very ground she walks on."

"Does she love you?"

"Oh, Lord, I don't know now. I thought so. She said she did. But she wouldn't . . . She promised to marry me. Watrous wants her settled. If she will marry me, I know I can make her love me."

"Never if you continued to be a two-faced, dirty, lousy, yellow dog of a horse thief," cried Dale forcefully. "You've got to perform a miracle. You've got to change. That's the price of my silence."

"Dale, I'm torn apart. . . . What use to swear? You know I'll quit—and go straight all my life. For Edith! What man wouldn't? You would if she gave herself. . . . Any man would. Don't you see that?"

"Yes, I see that, an' I believe you," replied Dale, convinced of the truth in Hildrith's agony. "I'll keep your secret, an' find a way to save you if any unforeseen things crop up. . . . An' that squares me with you, Leale Hildrith."

Swift light footsteps that scattered the gravel cut short Hildrith's impassioned gratitude. Edith startled Dale by appearing before them, her hand at her breast, her face white as a sheet, her eyes blazing.

Hildrith met her on the incline, exclaiming, "Why, Edith! Running back like that! What's wrong?"

She paid no heed to him, but ran to Dale, out of breath and visibly shaking.

"Oh—Dale—" she panted. "Stafford sent—for the sheriff! They're going to—arrest you."

"Stafford? Who's he? That man in the black coat?"

"Yes. He's lately—got in with Dad. . . . Cattle. It's his outfit of cowboys coming. . . . He's hard as nails."

"Are they here?"

"Will be—directly. I tore loose from Dad—and ran all the way. . . . Oh, Dale, what will you do?" She was unconscious of her emotion—and she put an appealing hand upon Dale's arm. Dale had never seen her like that, nor had Hildrith. They were deeply struck, each according to his reception of her white-faced, earnest demeanor.

"Edith, you can bet I won't run," declared Dale grimly. "Thank you, girl, all the same. . . . Don't take this so—so strangely. Why, you're all upset. They can't arrest me."

Hildrith drew back from the wide door. He appeared no less alarmed and excited than Edith. "They're coming, Dale," he said thickly. "Bayne and Stafford in the lead . . . That sheriff has it for you, Dale. Only last night I heard him swear he'd jail you if you came back. . . . It's ticklish business. What'll you do?"

"I'm sure I don't know," returned Dale with a laugh.

Edith besought him, "Oh, Dale, don't kill Bayne! . . . For my sake!"

"If you brace up, I reckon maybe I can avoid that." Dale led his horse out of the barn, down the runway into the open. Then he stepped aside to face the advancing men, now nearly across the wide court. The dark-garbed Stafford was talking and gesticulating vehemently to a stalwart booted man. This was the one officer that Salmon supported, and it had been said of him that he knew which side of the law to be on. Watrous and three other men brought up the rear. They made no bones about sheering off to the side. Stafford, however, a swarthy and pompous man, evidently accustomed to authority, remained beside Bayne.

"Hey, you," called out Dale, far from civilly. "If you want to talk with me—that's close enough."

Hildrith, to Dale's surprise, came down the incline, and took up a stand beside Dale.

"What you mean by this turkey-strutting?" he demanded, and his simulation of resentment would have deceived anyone but Dale.

"Hildrith, we got business with Brittenham," declared Bayne harshly.

"Well, he's my friend, and that concerns me."

"Thanks, Leale," interposed Dale. "But let me handle this. Bayne, are you lookin' for me?"

"I sure am."

"At whose instigation?"

"Mr. Stafford, here. He sent for me, an' he orders you arrested."

Watrous broke in to say nervously, "Brittenham, I advised against this. I have nothing to do with it. I don't approve of resorting to law on the strength of gossip. If you'll deny any association with horse thieves, that will do for me. If your word is good to Edith, it ought to be for me."

"Jim Watrous, you're a fool," rasped out Stafford. "Your daughter is apparently infatuated with this—this . . ."

"Careful!" cut in Dale. "You might say the wrong thing. An' leave Miss Edith's name out of this deal. . . . Stafford, what's your charge against me?"

"I think you're one of this horse-raiding gang," declared Stafford stoutly, though he turned pale.

"On what grounds?"

"I wasn't influenced by gossip, sir. I base my

suspicion on your fetching back those thoroughbred horses. They must have been driven off by mistake. Any horse thief would know they couldn't be ridden or sold in Montana or Idaho. They'd be recognized. So you fetched them back because it was good business. Besides, it'd put you in better with Watrous, and especially his—"

"Shut up! If you speak of that girl again I'll shoot your leg off," interrupted Dale. "An' you can gamble on this, Stafford. If I don't shoot you anyhow it'll be the only peg on which you can hang a doubt of my honesty."

"You insolent ruffian!" ejaculated Stafford, enraged and intimidated. "Arrest him, Sheriff."

"Brittenham, you'll have to come with me," spoke up Bayne with an uneasy cough. "You appear to be a talker. You'll get a chance to talk in court at Twin Falls."

"You're tryin' to go through with it?" asked Dale derisively.

"I say you're under arrest."

"What's *your* charge?"

"Same as Mr. Stafford's."

"But that's ridiculous, Bayne. You can't arrest a man for bringing back stolen horses. There's not the slightest case against me. Stafford has heard gossip in town—where half the population is crooked. How do I know an' how do *you* know that Stafford himself is not the big hand in this horse-stealin' gang? There's some big respectable rancher on this range who stands in with the thieves. Why do you pick on a poor wild-horse hunter? A ragamuffin, as he has called me. Look at my boots! Look at my saddle! If I was the go-between, wouldn't I have better equipment? You're not very bright, Bayne."

"Aw, thet's all bluff. Part of your game. An'

you've sure pulled it clever around here for three years."

While Dale had prolonged this argument, his mind had been conceiving and fixing upon a part he wanted to play. It would have been far easier but for Edith's inexplicable importunity. She had awakened something strange and hitherto unrevealed. It must have been pity, and real sincerity and regret come too late. Then the girl had always been fair in judging something between others. If Dale had had an inkling it was anything else, he never could have made the sacrifice, not even to save Hildrith. But she loved Hildrith; she would become his wife, and that surely meant his salvation. Dale felt that ignominy, a bad name thrust upon him and acknowledged by his actions, could not make much difference to him. He was only a wild-horse hunter. He could ride away to Arizona and never be heard of again. Still he hated the thing he felt driven to do.

Then Edith stepped into the foreground, no longer the distraught girl who had arrived there a few moments ago to warn Dale. Had she read his mind? That suspicion affected him more stirringly than anything yet that had happened.

"Sheriff Bayne, you must not try to arrest Dale without proof," she said earnestly.

"I'm sorry, lady. It's my duty. He'll get a fair trial."

"Fair!" exclaimed the girl scornfully. "When this arrest is so unfair! Bayne, there's something wrong—something dishonest here—and it's not in Dale."

"Edith, don't say more," interposed her father. "You're overwrought."

Hildrith strode to her side, hurried in manner, dark and strained of face.

"Leale, why don't you speak up for Dale?" she

queried, and her eyes blazed upon him with a marvelously penetrating and strange look.

"Bayne, let Dale off," Hildrith said huskily. "Don't make a mistake here. You've no proof—and you can't arrest him."

"Can't! Why the hell can't I?" rejoined the sheriff.

"Because he won't let you. Good God, man, haven't you any mind?"

"Humph! I've got mind enough to see there's somethin' damn funny here. But it ain't in me. . . . Brittenham, you're under arrest. Come on, now, no buckin'."

As he made a step forward Dale's gun gleamed blue and menacing.

"Look out, Bayne! If you move a hand I'll kill you," he warned.

He backed cautiously down the court, leading his horse to one side.

"I see what I'm up against here, an' I'm slopin'," went on Dale. "Stafford, you had it figured. Watrous, I engineered thet raid. . . . Edith, I fetched your horses back because I was in love with you." A strange laugh followed his words.

Dale backed across the square to the lane, where he leaped into his saddle and spurred swiftly out of sight.

•2•

DALE'S CAMPFIRE THAT NIGHT WAS ON A BEND OF THE brook near where he had surprised the three horse thieves, and had recovered the Watrous thoroughbreds.

Upon riding away from the Watrous ranch he had halted in Salmon long enough to buy supplies, then he had proceeded down the river to a lonely place where he had rested his horse and slept. By dawn he was climbing the mountain into Montana and by sundown that night he was far down the horse-thief trail.

Notwithstanding the fact that Dale had branded himself by shouldering Hildrith's guilt, he had determined to find Big Bill Mason's rendezvous and evolve a plan to break up the horse-thief band. Born of his passion at riding away from the Watrous ranch a fugitive, leaving Edith to regret her faith in him, this plan seemed to loom as gigantic and impossible after the long hours of riding and thinking. But he would not abandon it.

"Stafford and Bayne will send a big outfit after me," he muttered as he sat before his little campfire. "An' I'll lead them to Mason's hiding place. Failin' thet, I'll go down on the range below Bannock an' get the ranchers there to raise a big posse of cowboys. One way or another I'm goin' to break up Mason's gang."

Dale had not thought of that in the hour of his sacrifice for Hildrith and Edith. He had meant to take his friend's ignominy and ride away from Idaho forever. But two things had operated against this—first, the astounding and disturbing fact that Edith Watrous, in her stress of feeling, had betrayed not only faith in him but more real friendship than she had ever shown; and second, his riding away in disgrace would leave the Mason gang intact, free to carry on their nefarious trade. He was the man for the job. If he broke up the gang, it would remove the stain from his name. Not that he would ever want to or dare to go back to the Watrous ranch! But there was a tremendous force in the thought that he might stand clean and fine again in Edith Watrous's sight. How strangely she had reacted to that situation when her father and the others had confronted him! What could she have meant when she said there was something wrong, something dishonest there in that climax? Could she have had a glimmering of the truth? This thought was so disturbing that it made Dale catch his breath. Edith was a resourceful, strong-minded girl, once she became aroused. On reflection, however, he eased away that doubt, and also the humanly weak joy at a possible indestructible faith in him. No! He felt sure Hildrith would be safe. Once the Mason outfit was broken up, with the principals killed and the others run out of the country, Hildrith would be safe, and Edith's happiness would be assured.

In hours past, Dale had, in the excitement of his flight, believed that he could kill his love for Edith Watrous and forget her. This proved to be an illusion, the recognition of which came to him beside his lonely campfire. He would love her more, because his act had been something big and for her sake, and in his secret heart he would know that if she could be told the truth, she would see her faith justified, and whatever feeling she had for him would be intensified.

He saw her dark proud eyes and her white face in the opal glow of his fire. And having succumbed to that he could not help but remember her boldness to reward him, her arms and her kiss and, most poignant of all, the way she had been betrayed by her impulse, how that kiss had trapped her into this chance for Edith Watrous and she had never divined it? The thought was torture, and he put it from him, assuring himself that the girl's actions had been the result of her gratitude and joy at the return of her beloved horses.

The fire died down to ruddy coals; the night wind began to seep through the grass and brush; four-footed prowlers commenced their questing. A brooding solitude lay upon the forest.

He made his bed close under the side of a fallen pine, using his saddle for a pillow. So many nights of his life he had lain down to look up at the open dark sky with its trains of stars. But this night the stars appeared closer and they seemed to talk to him. He was conscious that his stern task, and the circumstances which had brought it about, had heightened all his faculties to a superlative degree. He seemed a vastly different man, and he conceived that it might develop that he would revel in what fate had set him to do.

At last he fell asleep. During the night he awoke several times, and the last time, which was near dawn and nippingly cold, he got up and kindled a fire. All about him rose dark gray forest wall, except in the east, where a pale brightening betokened dawn.

It was Dale's custom to cook and eat a hearty breakfast, so that he could go long on this meal if he had to. His last task before saddling was to obliterate signs of his camp. Then, with light enough to see clearly, he mounted and was off on his perilous quest.

All the way Dale had kept off the main trail. It would take an Indian or a wild-horse hunter to track him. He traveled some few paces off the horse-thief trail, but kept it in sight. And every mile or so he would halt, dismount, and walk a few steps away from his horse to listen. In that silent forest he could have heard a sound at a considerable distance.

By sunrise he was down out of the heavy timber belt and riding out upon a big country of scaly rock and immense thickets of evergreen and cedar, with only an occasional large pine. The brook disappeared—probably dried up, or sunk into the earth. The trail led on straight as a beeline, for a while.

The sun rose high, and grew hot. With the morning half spent, he figured that he had traveled fifteen miles from his last camp. Occasionally he had glimpses of the lower range, gray and vast and dim below. The trail turned west, into more rugged plateaus and away from the descent. But presently, beyond a long fringe of evergreen thicket, he saw the peculiar emptiness that proclaimed the presence of a void.

Dale knew before he reached it that he had come upon the hole in the ground where Big Bill Mason had his hideout. Leaving the proximity of the trail, Dale rode to a higher ground, where a gray stone eminence, less thickly overgrown, seemed to offer easy access to the place. Here he dismounted and pushed his way through the evergreens. At once he emerged upon a point, suddenly to stand rooted to the spot.

"What a wonderful place!" he exclaimed, as he grasped the fact that his sight commanded. He stood upon the rim of a deep gorge a mile long and half as wide. On all sides, the walls sheered down a thousand feet, gray and craggy, broken and caverned, lined by green branches, and apparently unscalable. Of course trails led in and out of this hole, but Dale could not see where. The whole vast level bottomland was as green as an emerald. At each end, where the gorge narrowed, glistened a lake. All around the rims stood up a thick border of evergreens, which screened the gorge from every side. Hunters and riders could pass near there without ever guessing the presence of such a concealed pocket in the mountain plateau.

"Ahuh. No wonder Mason can steal horses wholesale," said Dale. "All he had to do was to hide his tracks just after he made a raid."

Dale reflected that the thieves had succeeded in this up to the present time. However, any good tracker could sooner or later find this rendezvous for resting and shifting droves of horses. Dale was convinced that Stafford and Watrous would send out a large outfit of riders as soon as they were available.

It struck Dale singularly that he could not see an animal or a cabin in the gorge below. But undoubtedly there were points not visible to him from this particular location. Returning to his horse, he decided to ride around the gorge to look for another trail.

He found, after riding for a while, that although the gorge was hardly more than three or four miles in circumference, to circle it on horseback or even on foot, a man would have to travel three times that far. There were canyon offshoots from the main valley and these had to be headed.

At the west side Dale found one almost as long as the gorge itself. But it was narrow. Here he discovered the first sign of a trail since he had left the main one. And this was small, and had never been traveled by a drove of horses. It led off to the south toward Bannock. Dale deliberated a moment. If he were to risk going down to investigate, this trail, about halfway between the lakes at each end, should be the one for him to take. Certainly it did not show much usage. At length he rode down, impelled by a force that seemed to hold less of reason than of presagement.

It grew steep in the notch and shady, following a precipitous watercourse. He had to get off and lead his horse. Soon trees and brush obstructed his view. The trail was so steep that he could not proceed slowly, and before he surmised that he was halfway down, he emerged into the open to see a beautiful narrow valley, richly green, enclosed by timbered slopes. A new cabin of peeled logs stood in the lee of the north side. He saw cattle, horses and finally a man engaged in building a fence. If Dale had encountered an individual laboring this way in any other locality he would have thought him a homesteader. It was indeed the most desirable place to homestead and ranch on a small scale that Dale had ever seen in his hunting trips.

The man saw Dale just about as quickly as Dale had seen him. Riding by the cabin, where a buxom woman and some children peeped out fearfully, Dale approached the man. He appeared to be a sturdy thickset farmer, bearded and sharp-eyed. He walked forward a few steps and stopped significantly near a shiny rifle leaning against the fence. When Dale got close enough, he recognized him.

"Well, Rogers, you son-of-a-gun! What're you doin' down here?"

"Brittenham! By all thet's strange. I might ask you the same," was the hearty reply, as he offered a horny hand. Two years before Dale had made the acquaintance of Rogers back in the Sawtooth range.

"When'd you leave Camus Creek?" he asked.

"This spring. Fine place, thet. But too cold. I was snowed in all winter. Sold out to a Mormon."

"How'd you happen to locate in here?"

"Just accident. I went to Bannock, an' from there to Halsey. Liked thet range country. But I wanted to be high, where I could hunt an' trap as well as homestead. One day I hit the trail leadin' in here. An' you bet I located pronto."

"Before ridin' out in the big valley?"

"Yes, but I saw it. What a range! This was big enough for me. If I'm not run out I'll get rich here in five years."

"Then you located before you found out you had neighbors?"

"What do you know about them?" queried Rogers, giving Dale a speculative glance.

"I know enough."

"Brittenham, I hope to heaven you're not in thet outfit."

"No. An' I hope the same of you. Have you got wise yet to Mason's way of operatin'?"

"Mason! You don't mean the rancher an' horse trader Bill Mason?"

"Same hombre. Big Bill—the biggest horse thief in this country."

"So help me—! If thet's true, who can a man trust?"

"It's true, Rogers, as you can find out for yourself by watchin'. Mason runs a big outfit. They split. One operates in Idaho, the other in Montana. They drive the stolen horses up here an' switch men an' herds. They sell the Montana stock over in Idaho an' the Idaho stock over on the Montana ranges."

"Hell you say! Big idee an' sure a bold one. I savvy now why these men politely told me to pull up stakes an' leave. But I had my cabin up an' my family here before they found out I'd located. Then I refused to budge. Reed, the boss of the outfit, rode down again last week. Offered to buy me out. I thought thet strange. But he didn't offer much, so I refused to sell. He said his boss didn't want any homesteaders in here."

"Rogers, they'll drive you out or kill you," said Dale.

"I don't believe it. They're bluffin'. If they murdered me it'd bring attention to this place. Nobody knows of it. I haven't told about it yet. My wife would, though, if they harmed me."

"This gang wouldn't hesitate to put you all out of the way. They just don't take you seriously yet. Think they can scare you out."

"Not me! Brittenham, how'd you come to know about this horse stealin' an' to find this hole?"

Dale told him about the theft of the Watrous thoroughbreds, how he had trailed the robbers up the mountain, what happened there, and lastly about the big raid that followed hard the same day.

"I'll tell you, Rogers. I got blamed for bein' the scout member of Mason's outfit. It made me sore.

I left Salmon in a hurry, believe me. My aim in findin' this hole is to organize a big posse of cowboys an' break up Mason's gang."

"Humph! You ain't aimin' to do much, atall."

"It'll be a job. There's no tellin' how many outfits Mason runs. It's a good bet thet his ranch outfit is honest an' don't suspect he's a horse thief. I'll bet he steals his own horses. If I can raise a hard-fightin' bunch an' corral Mason's gang all here in this hole . . . To catch them here—thet's the trick. I'd reckon they'll be stragglin' in soon. It doesn't take long to sell a bunch of good horses. They'd hide here, gamblin' an' livin' fat until time for another raid . . . Rogers, breakin' up this outfit is important to you. How'd you like to help me?"

"What could I do? Remember I'm handicapped with a wife an' two kids."

"No fightin' an' no risk for you. I'd plan for you to watch the valley, and have some kind of signs I could see from the rim to tell me when the gang is here."

"Get down an' come in," replied the homesteader soberly. "We'll talk it over."

"I'll stop a little while. But I mustn't lose time."

"Come set on the porch. Meet the wife an' have a bite to eat. . . . Brittenham, I think I'll agree to help you. As for signs . . . Do you see thet bare point of rock up on the rim? . . . There. It's the only place on the rim from which you can see my valley an' cabin. I've a big white cowhide thet I could throw over the fence. You could see it much farther than thet. If you did see it, you'd know the gang was here."

"Just the trick, Rogers. An' no risk to you," replied Dale with satisfaction. He unsaddled Hoofs and let him free on the rich grass. Then he accompanied Rogers to the cabin, where he spent a restful hour. When he left, Rogers walked with him to the trail. They understood one another and were in accord on the plan to break up Mason's band. Dale climbed on foot to the rim, his horse following, and then rode east to the point designated by the homesteader. Rogers watched for him and waved.

Across the canyon Dale located a curve in the wall which partly enclosed a large area black with horses. He saw cattle, too, and extensive gardens, and far up among the trees yellow cabins amidst the green. He rode back to Rogers's trail and headed for Bannock, keen and grim over his project.

The trail zigzagged gradually down toward lower country. Dale was always vigilant. No moving object escaped him. But there was a singular dearth of life along this scantily timbered eastern mountain slope. Toward late afternoon he found himself in broken country again, where the trail wound between foothills. It was dark when he rode into Bannock.

This town, like Salmon, was in the heyday of its productivity. And it was considerably larger. Gold and silver mining were its main assets, but there was some cattle trade, and extensive business in horses, and the providing of supplies for the many camps in the hills. Gambling halls of the period, with all their manifest and hidden evils, flourished flagrantly.

A miner directed Dale to a stable where he left his horse. Here he inquired about his Indian friend, Nalook. Then he went uptown to find a restaurant. He did not expect to meet anyone who knew him unless it was the Indian. Later that contingency would have to be reckoned with. Dale soon found a place to eat. Next to him at the lunch counter sat a red-faced cowboy who answered his greeting civilly.

"How's the hash here?" asked Dale.

"Fair to middlin' . . . Stranger hereabout, eh?"

"Yep. I hail from the Snake River country."

"I see you're a range rider, but no cowman."

"You're a good guesser. My job is horses."

"Bronco buster, I'll bet."

"Nope. But I can an' do break wild horses."

"Reckon you're on your way to Halsey. There's a big sale of Idaho stock there tomorrow."

"Idaho horses. You don't say?" ejaculated Dale, pretending surprise. "I hadn't heard of it."

"Wal, I reckon it wasn't advertised over your way," replied the cowboy with a short laugh. "An' when you buy fine horses at half their value, you don't ask questions."

"Cowboy, you said a lot. I'm goin' to have a look at thet bunch. How far to Halsey?"

"Two hours for you, if you stretch leather. It takes a buckboard four."

Dale then attended to the business of eating, but that did not keep his mind from functioning actively. It staggered him to think that it was possible Mason had the brazen nerve to sell stolen Idaho horses not a hundred miles across the line.

"How about buckin' the tiger?" asked Dale's acquaintance as they went out into the street.

"No gamblin' for me, cowboy. I like to look on, though, when there's some big bettin'."

"I seen a game today. Poker. Big Bill Mason won ten thousand at Steens. You should have heard him roar. 'Thet pays up for the bunch of hosses stole from me the other day!' "

"Who's Big Bill Mason?" asked Dale innocently.

"Wal, he's about the whole cheese down Halsey way. Got his hand in most everythin'. I rode for him a spell."

"Does he deal much in horses?"

"Not so much as with cattle. But he always runs four or five hundred haid on his ranch."

Presently Dale parted from the cowboy and strolled along the dimly lighted street, peering into the noisy saloons, halting near groups of men, and listening. He spent a couple of hours that way, here and there picking up bits of talk. No mention of the big steal of Idaho horses came to Dale's ears. Still, with a daily stagecoach between the towns it was hardly conceivable that some news had not sifted through to Bannock.

Before leaving town, Dale bought a new shirt and a scarf. He slept that night in the barn where he had his horse put up. A pile of hay made a better bed than Dale usually had. But for a disturbing dream about Edith Watrous, in which she visited him in jail, he slept well. Next morning he shaved, and donned his new garments, after which he went into the town for breakfast. He was wary this morning. Early though the hour, the street was dotted with vehicles, and a motley string of pedestrians passed to and fro on the sidewalks.

Dale had a leisurely and ample breakfast, after which he strolled down the street to the largest store and entered, trying to remember what it was that he had wanted to purchase.

"Dale!" A voice transfixed him. He looked up to be confronted by Edith Watrous.

A red-cheeked, comely young woman accompanied Edith, and looked at Dale with bright, curious eyes.

He stammered confusedly in answer to Edith's greeting.

"Susan, this is my friend Dale Brittenham." Edith introduced him hurriedly. "Dale—Miss Bradford. . . . I came over here to visit Susan."

"Glad to meet you, Miss," returned Dale, doffing his sombrero awkwardly.

"I've heard about you," said the girl, smiling at Dale. But evidently she saw something was amiss for she turned to Edith and said, "You'll want to talk. I'll run do my buying."

"Yes, I want to talk to my friend Dale Brittenham," agreed Edith seriously. Her desire to emphasize the word "friend" could not be mistaken. She drew him away from the entrance of the store to a more secluded space. Then: "Dale!" Her voice was low and full of suppressed emotion. Pale, and with eyes dark with scorn and sorrow, she faced him.

"How'd you come over here?" he queried, regaining his coolness.

"Nalook drove me in the buckboard. He returned to the ranch after you left. We got here last night."

"I'm sorry you had the bad luck to run into me."

"Not bad luck, Dale. I followed you. I was certain you'd come here. There's no other town to go to."

"Followed me? Edith, what for?"

"Oh, I don't know—yet. . . . After you left I had a quarrel with Leale and Dad. I upbraided them for not standing by you. I swore you couldn't be a horse thief. I declared you were furious—that in your bitterness you just helped them to think badly of you."

"How could they help that when I admitted my—my guilt?"

"They couldn't—but *I* could. . . . Dale, I know you. If you had been a real thief, you'd never—never have told me you loved me that last terrible moment. You couldn't. You wanted me to know. You looked bitter—hard—wretched. There was nothing low-down or treacherous about you."

"Edith there you're wrong," returned Dale hoarsely. "For there is."

"Dale! Don't kill my faith in you. . . . Don't kill something I'm afraid . . ."

"It's true—to my shame an' regret."

"Oh! . . . So that's why you never made love to me like the other boys? You were man enough for that, at least. I'm indebted to you. But I'll tell you what I've found out. If you had been the splendid fellow I thought you—and if you'd had sense enough to tell me sooner that you loved me—well—there was no one I liked better, Dale Brittenham."

"My God—Edith, don't—I beg you—don't say thet now," implored Dale, in passionate sadness.

"I care a great deal for Leale Hildrith, but it was Dad's match. I told Leale so. I would probably have come to it of my own accord in time. Yesterday we had a quarrel. He made an awful fuss about my leaving home, so I slipped away unseen. But I'll bet he's on the way here right now."

"I hope he comes after you," said Dale, bewildered and wrenched by this disclosure.

"He'd better not. . . . Never mind him, Dale. You've hurt me. Perhaps I deserved it. For I have been selfish and vain with my friends. To find out you're a thief—Oh, I hate you for making me believe it! It's just sickening. But you can't—you simply can't become callous. You always had queer notions about range horses being free. There are no fences in parts of Idaho. Oh, see how I make excuses for you! Dale, promise me you will never help to steal another horse so long as you live."

Dale longed to fall upon his knees to her and tell her the truth. She was betraying more than she knew. He had seen her audacious and winning innumerable times, and often angry, and once eloquent, but never so tragic and beautiful as now. It almost broke down his will. He had to pull his hand from hers—to force a hateful stand utterly foreign to his nature.

"Edith, I won't lie to you—"

"I'm not sure of that," she retorted, her eyes piercing him. They had an intense transparency through which her thought, her doubt, shone like a gleam.

"Nope. I can't promise. My old wild-horse business is about played out. I've got to live."

"Dale, I'll give—lend you money, so you can go away far and begin all over again. Please, Dale?"

"Thanks, lady," he returned, trying to be laconic. "Sure I couldn't think of thet."

"You're so strange, so different. You didn't used to be like this. . . . Dale, is it my fault you went to the bad?"

"Nonsense!" he exclaimed in sudden heat. "Reckon it was just in me."

"Swear you're not lying to me."

"All right, I swear."

"If I believed I was to blame, I'd follow you and *make* you honest. I ought to do it anyhow."

"Edith, I'd have stayed away longer," said Susan, her eyes upon them. "Only, if we're going to Halsey we must rustle pronto."

"Edith, are you drivin' over there?" asked Dale quickly.

"Yes. Susan's brother is coming. There's a big horse sale on. I'm just curious to see if there will be any of Dad's horses there."

"I'm curious about that, too," admitted Dale soberly. "Good-bye, Edith. . . . Miss Bradford, glad to meet you, an' good-bye."

Dale strode swiftly out of the store, though Edith's call acted upon him like a magnet. Once outside, with restraint gone, he fell in a torment. He could not think coherently, let alone reason. That madcap girl, fully aroused, might be capable of anything. Dale suffered anguish as he rushed down the street and to the outskirts of town, where he saddled his horse and rode away down the slope to the east. There were both horsemen and vehicles going in the same direction, which he surmised as toward Halsey. Dale urged his mount ahead of them and then settled down to a steady sharp gait. He made no note of time, or the passing country. Long before noon he rode into Halsey.

The town appeared to be deserted, except for clerks in stores, bartenders at the doors of saloons, and a few loungers. Only two vehicles showed down the length of the long street. Dale did not need to ask why, but he did ask to be directed to the horse fair. He was not surprised to find a couple of hundred people, mostly men, congregated at the edge of town, where in an open green field several score of horses, guarded by mounted riders, grazed and bunched in front of the spectators. Almost the first horse he looked at twice proved to be one wearing the Watrous brand.

Then Dale had a keen eye for that drove of horses and especially the horsemen. In a country where all men packed guns, their being armed did not mean anything to casual observers. Nevertheless to Dale it was significant. They looked to him to be a seasoned outfit of hard riders. He hid Hoofs in the background and sauntered over toward the center of activities.

"Where's this stock from?" he asked one of a group of three men, evidently ranchers, who were bystanders like himself.

"Idaho. Snake River range."

"Sure some fine saddle hosses," went on Dale. "What they sellin' for?"

"None under a hundred dollars. An' goin' like hotcakes,"

"Who's the hoss dealer?"

"Ed Reed. Hails from Twin Falls."

"Ahuh. Gentlemen, I'm a stranger in these parts," said Dale deliberately. "I hear there's no end of hoss business goin' on—hoss sellin', hoss buying', hoss tradin'—and' *hoss stealin'*."

"Wal, this is a hoss country," spoke up another of the trio dryly, as he looked Dale up and down. Dale's cool speech had struck them significantly.

"You got all the earmarks of range men," Dale continued curtly. "I'd like to ask, without 'pearin' too inquisitive, if any one of you has lost stock lately?"

There followed a moment of silence, in which the three exchanged glances and instinctively edged close together.

"Wal, stranger, I reckon thet's a fair question," replied the eldest, a gray-haired, keen-eyed Westerner. "Some of us ranchers down in the range have been hit hard lately."

"By what? Fire, flood, blizzard, drought—or hoss thieves?"

"I reckon thet last, stranger. But don't forget you said it."

"Fine free country, this, where a range man can't talk right out," rejoined Dale caustically. "I'll tell you why. You don't know who the hoss thieves are. An' particular, their chief. He might be one of your respectable rancher neighbors."

"Stranger, you got as sharp a tongue as eye," returned the third member of the group. "What's your name an' what's your game?"

"Brittenham. I'm a wild-horse hunter from the

Snake River Basin. My game is to get three or four tough cowboy outfits together."

"Wal, thet oughtn't be hard to do in this country, if you had reason," returned the rancher, eyes narrowing. Dale knew he did not need to tell these men that the drove of horses before them had been stolen.

"I'll look you up after the sale," he concluded.

"My name's Strickland. We'll sure be on the lookout for you."

The three moved on toward the little crowd near the horses at that moment under inspection. "Jim, if we're goin' to buy some stock we've got to hustle," remarked one.

Dale sauntered away to get a good look at the main drove of horses. When he recognized Dusty Dan, a superb bay that he had actually straddled himself, a bursting gush of hot blood burned through his veins. Deliberately he stepped closer, until he was halted by one of the mounted guards.

"Whar you goin', cowboy?" demanded this individual, a powerful rider of matured years, clad in greasy leather chaps and dusty blouse. He had a bearded visage and deep-set eyes, gleaming under a black sombrero pulled well down.

"I'm lookin' for my hoss," replied Dale mildly.

The guard gave a slight start, barely perceptible.

"Wal, do you see him?" he queried insolently.

"Not yet."

"What kind of hoss, cowboy?"

"He's a black with white face. Wearin' a *W* brand like that bay there. He'd stand out in thet bunch like a silver dollar in a fog."

"Wal, he ain't hyar, an' you can mosey back."

"Hell you say," retorted Dale, changing his demeanor in a flash. "These horses are on inspection. . . . An' see here, Mr. Leather Pants, don't tell *me* to mosey anywhere."

Another guard, a lean, sallow-faced man, rode up to query, "Who's this guy, Jim?"

"Took him for a smart-alec cowboy."

"You took me wrong, you Montana buckaroos," interposed Dale, cool and caustic. "I'll mosey around an' see if I can pick out a big black hoss with the *W* brand."

Dale strode on, but he heard the guard called Jim mutter to his companion, "Tip Reed off." Presently Dale turned in time to see the rider bend from his saddle to speak in the ear of a tall dark man. Thus Dale identified Ed Reed, and without making his action marked, he retraced his steps. On his way he distinguished more *W* brands and recognized more Watrous horses.

Joining the group of buyers, Dale looked on from behind. After one survey of Big Bill Mason's right-hand man Dale estimated him to be a keen, suave villain whose job was to talk, but who would shoot on the slightest provocation.

"Well, gentlemen, we won't haggle over a few dollars," Reed was saying blandly as he waved a hairy brown hand. "Step up and make your offers. These horses have got to go."

Then buying took on a brisk impetus. During the next quarter of an hour a dozen and more horses were bought and led away, among them Dusty Dan. That left only seven animals, one of which was the white-faced black Dale had spoken about to the guard, but had not actually seen.

"Gentlemen, here's the pick of the bunch," spoke up Reed. "Eight years old. Sound as a rock. His sire was blooded stock. I forget the name. What'll you offer?"

"Two hundred fifty," replied a young man eagerly.

"That's a start. Bid up, gentlemen. This black is gentle, fast, wonderful gait. A single-footer. You see how he stacks up."

"Three hundred," called Dale, who meant to outbid any other buyers, take the horse and refuse to pay.

"Come on. Don't you Montana men know horseflesh when . . ."

Reed halted with a violent start and the flare of his eyes indicated newcomers. Dale wheeled with a guess that he verified in the sight of Edith Watrous and Leale Hildrith, with another couple behind them. He also saw Nalook, the Indian, at the driver's seat of the buckboard. Hildrith's face betrayed excessive emotion under control. He tried to hold Edith back. But, resolute and pale, she repelled him and came on. Dale turned swiftly so as not to escape Reed's reaction to this no doubt astounding and dangerous interruption. Dale was treated to an extraordinary expression of fury and jealousy. It passed from Reed's dark glance and dark face as swiftly as it had come.

Dale disliked the situation that he saw imminent. There were ten in Reed's gang—somber, dark-browed men, whom it was only necessary for Dale to scrutinize once to gauge their status. On the other hand the majority of spectators and buyers were not armed. Dale realized that he had to change his mind, now that Edith was there. To start a fight would be foolhardy and precarious.

The girl had fire in her eyes as she addressed the little group.

"Who's boss here?" she asked.

"I am, Miss. . . . Ed Reed, at your service." Removing his sombrero he made her a gallant bow. His face was strong and not unhandsome in a bold way. Certainly his gaze was one of unconcealed admiration.

"Mr. Reed, that black horse with the white face belongs to me," declared Edith imperiously.

"Indeed?" replied Reed, exhibiting apparently genuine surprise. "And who're you, may I ask?"

"Edith Watrous. Jim Watrous is my father."

"Pleased to meet you. . . . You'll excuse me, Miss Watrous, if I ask for proof that this black is yours."

Edith came around so that the horse could see her, and she spoke to him. "Dick, old boy, don't you know me?"

The black pounded the ground, and with a snort jerked the halter from the man who held him. Whinnying, he came to Edith, his fine eyes soft, and he pressed his nose into her hands.

"There! . . . Isn't that sufficient?" asked Edith.

Reed had looked on with feigned amusement. Dale gauged him as deep and resourceful.

"Sam, fetch my hoss. I'm tired of standing and I reckon this lady has queered us for other buyers."

"Mr. Reed. I'm taking my horse whether you like it or not," declared Edith forcefully.

"But, Miss Watrous, you can't do that. You haven't proved to me he belongs to you. I've seen many fine horses that'd come to a woman."

"Where did you get Dick?"

"I bought him along with the other *W* brand horses."

"From whom?" queried Edith derisively.

"John Williams. He's a big breeder in horses. His ranch is on the Snake River. I daresay your father knows him."

Dale stepped out in front. "Reed, there's no horse breeder on the Snake River," he said.

The horse thief coolly mounted a superb bay that had been led up, and then gazed sardonically from Edith to Dale.

"Where do you come in?"

"My name is Brittenham. I'm a wild-horse hunter. I know every foot of range in the Snake between the falls an' the foothills."

"Williams's ranch is way up in the foothills," rejoined Reed easily. He had not exactly made a perceptible sign to his men, but they had closed in, and two of them slipped out of their saddles. Dale could not watch them and Reed at the same time. He grew uneasy. These thieves, with their crafty and bold leader, were masters of the situation.

"Lady, I hate to be rude, but you must let go that halter," said Reed, with an edge on his voice.

"I won't."

"Then I'll have to be rude. Sam, take that rope away from her."

"Leale, say something, can't you? What kind of a man are you, anyway?" cried Edith, turning in angry amazement to her fiancé.

"What can I say?" asked Hildrith, spreading wide his hands, as if helpless. His visage at the moment was not prepossessing.

"What! Why tell him you know this is my horse."

Reed let out a laugh that had bitter satisfaction as well as irony in it. Dale had to admit that the predicament for Hildrith looked extremely serious.

"Reed, if Miss Watrous says it's her horse, you can rely on her word," replied the pallid Hildrith.

"I'd take no woman's word," returned the leader.

"Dale, you know it's my horse. You've ridden him. If you're not a liar, Mr. Reed knows you as well as you know me."

"Excuse me, lady," interposed Reed. "I never

saw your wild-horse hunter champion in my life. If he claims to know me, he is a liar."

"Dale!" Edith transfixed him with soul-searching eyes.

"I reckon you forget, Reed. Or you just won't own up to knowin' me. Thet's no matter. . . . But the horse belongs to Miss Watrous. I've ridden him. I've seen him at the Watrous ranch every day or so for years."

"Brittenham. Is that what you call yourself? I'd lie for her, too. She's one grand girl. But she can't rob me of this horse."

"Rob! That's funny, Mr. Reed," exclaimed Edith hotly. "You're the robber! I'll bet Dick against two bits that *you're* the leader of this horse-thief gang."

"Well, I can't shoot a girl, much less such a pretty and tantalizing one as you. But don't say that again. I might forget my manners."

"You brazen fellow!" cried Edith, probably as much incensed by his undisguised and bold gaze as by his threat. "I not only think you're a horse thief, but I call you one!"

"All right. You can't be bluffed, Edith," he returned grimly. "You've sure got nerve. But you'll be sorry, if it's the last trick I pull on this range."

"Edith, get away from here," ordered Hildrith huskily, and he plucked at her with shaking hands. "Let go that halter."

"No!" cried Edith, fight in every line of her face and form, and as she backed away from Hildrith, she inadvertently drew nearer to Reed.

"But you don't realize who—what this man . . ."

"Do you?" she flashed piercingly.

Dale groaned in spirit. This was the end of Leale Hildrith. The girl was as keen as a whip and bristling with suspicion. The unfortunate man almost cringed before her. Then Reed rasped out, "*Rustle there!*"

At the instant that Reed's ally Sam jerked the halter out of Edith's hand, Dale felt the hard prod of a gun against his back. "Put 'em up, Britty," called a surly voice. Dale lost no time getting his hands above his head and he cursed under his breath for his haste and impetuosity. He was relieved of his gun. Then the pressure on his back ceased.

Reed reached down to lay a powerful left hand on Edith's arm.

"Let go!" the girl burst out angrily, and she struggled to free herself. "Oh, you hurt me! Stop, you ruffian."

"Stand still, girl!" he ordered, trying to hold her and the spirited horse. "He'll step on you—crush your foot."

"Ah-h!" screamed Edith, in agony, as she ceased her violent exertion to stand limp, holding up one foot. The red receded from her face.

"Take your hand off her," shouted Hildrith, reaching for a gun that was not there.

"Is that your stand, Hildrith?" queried Reed, cold and hard.

"What do you mean?"

"It's a showdown. This jig is up. Show yellow—or come out with the truth before these men. Don't leave it to me."

"Are you drunk—or crazy?" screamed Hildrith, beside himself. He did not grasp Reed's deadly intent, whatever his scheme was. He thought his one hope was to play his accustomed part. Yet he suspected a move that made him frantic.

"Let her go! . . . Damn your black hide—let her go!"

"Black, but not yellow, you traitor!" wrung out Reed as he leveled a gun at Hildrith. "We'll see what the boss says to this. . . . Rustle, or I'll kill you. I'd like to do it. But you're not my man. . . . Get over there quick. Put him on a horse, men, and get going. . . . Sam, up with her!"

Before Dale could have moved, even if he had been able to accomplish anything, unarmed as he was, the man seized Edith and threw her up on Reed's horse, where despite her struggles and cries he jammed her down in the saddle in front of Reed.

As Reed wheeled away, looking back with menacing gun, the spectators burst into a loud roar. Sam dragged the black far enough to be able to leap astride his own horse and spur away, pulling his captive into his stride. The other men, ahead of Reed, drove the unsaddled horses out in front. The swiftness and precision of the whole gang left the crowd stunned. They raced out across the open range, headed for the foothills. Edith's pealing cry came floating back.

•3•

DALE WAS THE FIRST TO RECOVER FROM THE SWIFT RAW shock of the situation. All around him milled an excited crowd. Most of them did not grasp the significance of the sudden exodus of the horse dealers until they were out sight. Dale, nearly frantic, lost no time in finding Strickland.

"Reckon I needn't waste time now convincin' you there are some horse thieves in this neck of the woods?" he spat out sarcastically.

"Brittenham, I'm plumb beat," replied the rancher, and he looked it. "In my ten years on this range I never saw the like of that. . . . My Gawd! What an impudent rascal! To grab the Watrous girl right under our noses! Not a shot fired!"

"Don't rub it in," growled Dale. "I had to watch Reed. His man got the drop on me. A lot of slick hombres. An' thet's not sayin' half."

"We'll hang every damn one of them," shouted Strickland.

"Yes. After we save the girl. . . . Step aside here with me. Fetch those men you had. . . . Come, both of you. . . . Now, Strickland, this is stern business. We've not a minute to waste. I want a bunch of hard-ridin' cowboys here *pronto*. Figure quick now, while I get my horse, an' find thet Indian."

Dale ran into the lithe, dark, buckskin clad Nalook as he raced for his horse. This Indian had no equal as a tracker in Idaho.

"Boss, you go me," Nalook said in his low voice, with a jerk of his thumb toward the foothills. Apparently the Indian had witnessed the whole action.

"Rustle, Nalook. Borrow a horse an' guns. I've got grub."

Dale hurried back, leading Hoofs. Reaching Strickland and his friends, he halted with them and waited, meanwhile taking his extra guns out of his pack.

"I can have a posse right here in thirty minutes," declared the rancher.

"Good. But I won't wait. The Indian here will go with me. We'll leave a trail they can follow on the run. Tracks an' broken brush."

"I can get thirty or more cowboys here in six hours."

"Better. Tell them the same."

Nalook appeared at his elbow. "Boss, me no find hoss."

"Strickland, borrow a horse for this Indian. I'll need him."

"Joe, go with the Indian," said Strickland. "Get him horse and outfit if you have to buy it."

"You men listen and hold your breath," whispered Dale. "This Reed outfit is only one of several. Their boss is Big Bill Mason."

The ranchers were beyond surprise or shock. Strickland snapped his fingers.

"That accounts. Dale, I'll tell you something. Mason got back to Halsey last night from Bannock, he said. He was not himself. This morning he sold his ranch—gave it away, almost—to Jeff Wheaton. He told Wheaton he was leaving Montana."

"Where is he now?"

"Must have left early. You can bet something was up for him to miss a horse sale."

"When did Reed's outfit arrive?"

"Just before noon."

"Here's what happened," Dale calculated audibly. "Mason must have heard thet Stafford an' Watrous was sendin' a big posse out on the trail of Mason's Idaho outfit."

"Brittenham, if this Ed Reed didn't call Hildrith to show his hand for or against that outfit, then I'm plumb daft."

"It looked like it," admitted Dale gloomily.

"I thought he was going to kill Hildrith."

"So did I. There's bad blood between them."

"Hildrith has had dealings of some kind with Reed. Remember how Reed spit out, 'We'll see what the boss says about this. . . . I'd like to kill you'? . . . Brittenham, I'd say Hildrith has fooled Watrous and his daughter, and this Mason outfit also."

Dale was saved from a reply by the approach of Nalook, mounted on a doughty mustang. He carried a carbine and wore a brass-studded belt with two guns.

"We're off, Strickland," cried Dale, kicking his stirrup straight and mounting. "Hurry your posse an' outfits. Pack light, an' rustle's the word."

Once out of the circle of curious onlookers, Dale told Nalook to take the horse thieves' trail and travel. The Indian pointed toward the foothills.

"Me know trail. Big hole. Indian live there long time. Nalook's people know hoss thieves."

"I've been there, Nalook. Did you know Bill Mason was chief of thet outfit?"

"No sure. See him sometime. Like beaver. Hard see."

"We'd better not shortcut. Sure Reed will make for the hideout hole. But he'll camp on the way."

"No far. Be there sundown."

"Is it that close from this side? . . . All the better. Lead on, Nalook. When we hit the brush we want to be close on Reed's heels."

The Indian followed Reed's tracks at a lope. They led off the grassy lowland toward the hills. Ten miles or more down on the range to the east Dale spied a ranch, which Nalook said was Mason's. At that distance it did not look pretentious. A flat-topped ranch house, a few sheds and corrals, and a few cattle dotting the grassy range inclined Dale to the conviction that this place of Mason's had served as a blind to his real activities.

Soon Nalook led off the rangeland into the foothills. Reed's trail could have been followed in the dark. It wound through ravines and hollows between hills that soon grew high and wooded on top. The dry wash gave place to pools of water here and there, and at last a running brook, lined by grass and willows growing green and luxuriant.

At length a mountain slope confronted the trackers. Here the trail left the watercourse and took a slant up the long incline. Dale sighted no old hoofmarks and concluded that Reed was making a shortcut to the rendezvous. At intervals Dale broke branches on the willows and brush he passed, and let them hang down, plainly visible to a keen eye. Rocks and brush, cactus and scrub oak grew increasingly manifest, and led to the cedars, which in turn yielded to the evergreens.

It was about midafternoon when they surmounted the first bench of the mountain. With a posse from Halsey possibly only a half hour behind, Dale slowed up the Indian. Reed's tracks were fresh in the red bare ground. Far across the plateau the belt of pines showed black, and the gray rock ridges stood up. Somewhere in that big rough country hid the thieves' stronghold.

"Foller more no good," said Nalook, and left Reed's tracks for the first time.

Dale made no comment. But he fell to hard pondering. Reed, bold outlaw that he was, would this time expect pursuit and fight, if he stayed in the country. His abducting the girl had been a desperate, unconsidered impulse, prompted by her beauty, or by desire for revenge on Hildrith, or possibly to hold her for ransom, or all of these together. No doubt he knew this easy game was up for Mason. He had said as much to Hildrith. It was not conceivable to Dale that Reed would stay in the country if Mason was leaving. They had made their big stake.

Nalook waited for Dale on the summit of a ridge. "Ugh!" he said, and pointed.

They had emerged near the head of a valley that bisected the foothills and opened out upon the range, dim and hazy below. Dale heard running water. He saw white flags of deer in the brush. It was a wild and quiet scene.

"Mason trail come here," said the Indian, with an expressive gesture downward.

Then he led on, keeping to the height of slope; and once over that, entered rough and thicketed land that impeded their progress. In many places the soft red and yellow earth gave way to stone, worn to every conceivable shape. There were hollows and upstanding grotesque slabs and cones, and long flat stretches, worn uneven by erosion. Evergreens and sage and dwarf cedars found lodgment in holes. When they crossed this area to climb higher and reach a plateau, the sun was setting gold over the black mountain heights. Dale recognized the same conformation of earth and rock that he had found on the south side of the robbers' gorge. Nalook's slow progress and caution brought the tight cold stretch to Dale's skin. They were nearing their objective.

At length the Indian got off his horse and tied it behind a clump of evergreens. Dale followed suit. They drew their rifles.

"We look—see. Mebbe come back," whispered Nalook. He glided on without the slightest sound or movement of foliage, Dale endeavoring to follow his example. After traversing half a mile in circuitous route, he halted and put a finger to his nose. "Smell smoke. Tobac."

But Dale could not catch the scent. Not long afterward, however, he made out the peculiar emptiness behind a line of evergreens and this marked the void they were seeking. They kept on at a snail's pace.

Suddenly Nalook halted and put a hand back to stop Dale. He could not crouch much lower. Warily he pointed over the fringe of low evergreens to a pile of gray rocks. On the summit sat a man with his back to the trackers. He was gazing intently in the opposite direction. This surely was a guard stationed there to spy any pursuers, presumably approaching on the trail.

"Me shoot him," whispered Nalook.

"I don't know," whispered Dale in reply, perplexed. "How far to their camp?"

"No hear gun."

"But there might be another man on watch."

"Me see."

The Indian glided away like a snake. How invaluable he was in a perilous enterprise like this! Dale sat down to watch and wait. The sun sank and shadows gathered under the evergreens. The scout on duty seemed not very vigilant. He never turned once to look back. But suddenly he stood up guardedly, and thrust his rifle forward. He took aim and appeared about to fire. Then he stiffened strangely, and jerked up as if powerfully propelled. Immediately there followed the crack of a rifle. Then the guard swayed and fell backward out of sight. Dale heard a low crash and a rattle of rocks. Then all was still. He waited. After what seemed a long anxious time, the thud of hoofs broke the silence. He sank down, clutching his rifle. But it was Nalook coming with the horses.

"We go quick. Soon night," said the Indian, and led the way toward the jumble of rocks. Presently Dale saw a trail as wide as a road. It led down. Next he got a glimpse of the gorge. From this end it was more wonderful to gaze down into, a magnificent hole, with sunset gilding the opposite wall, and purple shadows mantling the caverns, and the lake shining black.

Viewed from this angle Mason's rendezvous presented a different and more striking spectacle. This north end where Dale stood was a great deal lower than the south end, or at least the walls were lower and the whole zigzag oval of rims sloped toward him, so that he was looking up at the southern escarpments. Yet the floor of the gorge appeared level. From this vantage point the caverns and cracks in the walls stood out darkly and mysteriously, suggesting hidden places and perhaps unseen exits from this magnificent burrow. The deep indentation of the eastern side, where Mason had his camp, was not visible from any other point. At that sunset hour a mantle of gold and purple hung over the chasm. All about it seemed silent and secretive, a wild niche of nature, hollowed out for the protection of men as wild as the place. It brooded under the gathering twilight. The walls gleamed dark with a forbidding menace.

Nalook started down, leading his mustang. Then Dale noted that he had a gun belt and long silver spurs hung over the pommel of his saddle. He had taken time to remove these from the guard he had shot. This trail was open and from its zigzag corners Dale caught glimpses of the gorge, and of droves of horses. Suddenly he remembered that he had forgotten to break brush and otherwise mark their path after they had sheered off Reed's tracks.

"Hist!" he whispered. The Indian waited. "It's gettin' dark. Strickland's posse can't trail us."

"Ugh. They foller Reed. Big moon. All same day."

Thus reassured, Dale followed on, grimly fortifying himself to some issue near at hand.

When they came out into the open valley below, dusk had fallen. Nalook had been in that hole before, Dale made certain. He led away from the lake along a brook, and let his horse drink. Then he drank himself, and motioned Dale to do likewise. He went on then, in among scrub-oak trees to a grassy open spot where he halted.

"Mebbe long fight," he whispered. "I rope hoss." Dale removed saddle and bridle from Hoofs and tied him on a long halter.

"What do?" asked Nalook.

"Sneak up on them."

By this time it was dark down in the canyon, though still light above. Nalook led out of the trees and, skirting them, kept to the north wall. Presently he turned and motioned Dale to lift his feet, one after the other, to remove his spurs. The Indian hung them in the crotch of a bush. Scattered trees of larger size began to loom up on this higher ground. The great black wall stood up, rimmed with white stars. Dim lights glimmered through the foliage and gradually grew brighter. Nalook might have been a shadow for the sound he made. Intensely keen and vigilant as Dale was, he could not keep from swishing the grass or making an occasional rustle in the brush. Evidently the Indian did not want to lose time, but he kept cautioning Dale with an expressive backward gesture.

Nalook left the line of timber under the wall and took out into the grove. He now advanced more cautiously than ever. Dale thought his guide must have the eyes of a nighthawk. They passed a dark shack which was open in front and had a projecting roof. Two campfires were blazing a hundred yards farther on. And a lamp shone through what must have been a window of a cabin.

Presently the Indian halted. He pointed. Then Dale saw horses and men, and he heard gruff voices and the sound of flopping saddles. Some outfit had just arrived. Dale wondered if it was Reed's. If so, he had tarried some little time after getting down into the gorge.

"We look—see," whispered Nalook in Dale's ear. The Indian seemed devoid of fear. He seemed actuated by more than friendship for Dale and gratitude to Edith Watrous. He hated someone in that horse-thief gang.

Dale followed him, growing stern and hard. He could form no idea of what to do except get the lay of the land, ascertain if possible what Reed was up to, and then go back to the head of the trail and wait for the posse. But he well realized the precarious nature of spying on these desperate men. He feared, too, that Edith Watrous was in vastly more danger of harm than of being held for ransom.

The campfires lighted up two separate circles, both in front of the open-faced shacks. Around the farther one, men were cooking a meal. Dale smelled ham and coffee. The second fire had just been kindled and its bright blaze showed riders moving about still with chaps on, unsaddling and unpacking. Dale pierced the gloom for sight of Edith but failed to locate her.

The Indian sheered away to the right so that a cabin hid the campfires. This structure was a real log cabin of some pretensions. Again a lamp shone through a square window. Faint streaks of light, too, came from chinks between the logs. Dale tried to see through the window, but Nalook led him at a wrong angle. Soon they reached the cabin. Dale felt the rough peeled logs. Nalook had an ear against the log wall. No sound within! Then the Indian, moving with extreme stealth, slipped very slowly along the wall until he came to one of the open chinks. Dale suppressed his eagerness. He must absolutely move without a sound. But that was easy. Thick grass grew beside the cabin. In another tense moment Dale came up with Nalook, who clutched his arm and pulled him down.

There was an aperture between the logs where the mud filling had fallen out. Dale applied his eyes to the small crack. His blood leaped at the sight of a big man sitting at a table. Black-browed, scant-bearded, leonine Bill Mason! A lamp with a white globe shed a bright light. Dale saw a gun on the corner of the table, some buckskin sacks, probably containing gold, in front of Mason, and some stacks of greenbacks. An open canvas pack sat on the floor beside the table. Another pack, half full, and surrounded by articles of clothing, added to Dale's conviction that the horse-thief leader was preparing to leave this rendezvous. The dark frown on Mason's brow appeared to cast its shadow over his strong visage.

A woman's voice, high-pitched and sweet, coming through the open door of the cabin, rang stingingly on Dale's ears.

". . . I told you. . . . Keep your horsy hands off me. I can walk."

Mason started up in surprise. "A woman! Now what in hell?"

Then Edith Watrous, pale and worn, her hair disheveled and her dress so ripped that she had to hold it together, entered the cabin to fix dark and angry eyes upon the dual-sided rancher. Behind her, cool and sardonic, master of the situation, appeared Reed, blocking the door as if to keep anyone else out.

"Mr. Mason, I am Edith—Watrous," panted the girl.

"You needn't tell me. I know you. . . . What in the world are you doing here?" rejoined Mason slowly, as he arose to his commanding height. He exhibited dismay, but he was courteous.

"I've been—treated to an—outrage. I was in Halsey—visiting friends. There was a horse sale. . . . I went out. I found my horse Dick—and saw other Watrous horses in the bunch. . . . I promptly told this man Reed—it was my horse. He argued with me. . . . Then Hildrith came up—and that precipitated trouble. Reed put something up to Hildrith—I didn't get just what. But it looks bad. I thought he was going to kill Hildrith. But he didn't. He cursed Hildrith and said he'd see what the boss would do about it. . . . They threw me on Reed's horse—made me straddle his saddle in front—and I had to endure a long ride—with my dress up to my head—my legs exposed to brush—and what was more to—to the eyes of Reed and his louts. . . . It was terrible. . . . I'm so perfectly furious that—that—"

She choked in her impassioned utterance.

"Miss Watrous, I don't blame you," said Mason. "Please understand this is not my doing." Then he fastened his black angry eyes upon his subordinate. "Fool! What's your game?"

"Boss, I didn't have any," returned Reed coolly. "I just saw red. It popped into my head to make off with this stuck-up Watrous woman. And here we are."

"Reed, you're lying. You've got some deep game. . . . Jim Watrous was a friend of mine. I can't stand for such an outrage to his daughter."

"You'll have to stand it, Mason. You and I split, you know, over this last deal. It's just as I gambled would happen. You've ruined us. We're through."

"Ha! I can tell you as much."

"There's a wild-horse hunter down at Halsey—Dale Brittenham. I know about him. He's the man who trailed Ben, Alec and Steve—he killed them. He's on to us. I saw that. He'll have a hundred gunners on our trail by sunup."

"Ed, that's not half we're up against," replied the chief gloomily. "This homesteader Rogers, with his trail to Bannock—that settled our hash. Stafford and Watrous have a big outfit after us. I heard it at Bannock. That's why I sold out. I'm leaving here as soon as I can pack."

"Fine. That's like you. Engineered all the jobs and let us do the stealing while you hobnobbed with the ranchers you robbed. Now you'll leave us to fight. . . . Mason, I'm getting out too—and I'm taking the girl."

"Good God! Ed, it's bad enough to be a horse thief. But to steal a beautiful and well-connected girl like this. . . . Why man, it's madness! What for, I ask you?"

"That's my business."

"You want to make Watrous pay to get her back. He'd do it, of course, but he'd tear Montana to pieces, and hang you."

"I might take his money—later. But I confess to a weakness for the young lady. . . . And I'll get even with Hildrith."

"Revenge, eh? You always hated Leale. But what's he got to do with your game?"

"He's crazy in love with her. Engaged to marry her."

"He *was* engaged to me, Mr. Mason," interposed Edith scornfully. "I thought I cared for him. But I really didn't. I despise him now. I wouldn't marry him if he was the last man on earth."

"Reed, does she know?" asked Mason significantly.

"Well, she's not dumb, and I reckon she's got a hunch."

"I'll be—!" Whatever Mason's profanity was he did not give it utterance. "Hildrith! But we had plans to pull stakes and leave this country. Did he intend to marry Miss Watrous and bring her with us? . . . That's not conceivable."

"Boss, he cheated you. He never meant to leave."

Mason made a passionate gesture, as if to strike deep and hard, his big eyes rolled in a fierce glare. It was plain now to the watching Dale why Reed had wanted Hildrith to face his chief.

"Where's Hildrith?" growled Mason.

"Out by the fire under guard."

"Call him in." Reed went out.

Then Edith turned wonderingly and fearfully to Mason.

"Hildrith is *your* man!" She affirmed rather than queried.

"Yes, Miss Watrous, he was."

"Then *he* is the spy, the scout—the traitor who acted as go-between for you."

"Miss Watrous, he certainly has been my right-hand man for eight years. . . . And I'm afraid Reed and you are right about his being a traitor."

At that juncture Hildrith lunged into the cabin as if propelled viciously from behind. He was ashen-hued under his beard. Reed stamped in after him, forceful and malignant, sure of the issue. But just as Mason, after a steady hard look at his lieutenant, was about to address him, Edith flung herself in front of Hildrith.

"It's all told, Leale Hildrith," she cried, with a fury of passion. "Reed gave you away. Mason corroborated him. . . . *You* are the tool of these men. *You* were the snake in the grass. *You*, the liar who ingratiated himself into my father's confidence. Made love to me! Nagged me until I was beside myself! . . . But your wrong to me—your betrayal of Dad—these fall before your treachery to Dale Brittenham. . . . You let *him* take on your guilt. . . . Oh, I see it all now. It's ghastly. That man loved you . . . you despicable—despicable—"

Edith broke off, unable to find further words. With tears running down her colorless cheeks, her eyes magnificent with piercing fire, she manifestly enthralled Reed with her beauty and passion. She profoundly impressed Mason and she struck deep into what manhood the stricken Hildrith had left.

"All true, Bill, I'm sorry to confess," he said, his voice steady. "I'm offering no excuse. But look at her, man . . . look at her! And then you'll understand."

"What's that, Miss, about Dale Brittenham?" asked Mason.

"Brittenham's a wild-horse hunter," answered Edith, catching her breath. "Hildrith befriended him once. Dale love Hildrith. . . . When Stafford came to see Dad—after the last raid—he accused Dale of being the spy who kept your gang posted. The go-between. He had the sheriff come to arrest Dale. . . . Oh, I see it all now. Dale *knew* Hildrith was the traitor. He sacrificed himself for Hildrith—to pay his debt—or because he thought I loved the man. For us both! . . . He drew a gun on Bayne—said Stafford was right that *he* was the horse-thief spy . . . then he rode away."

It was a poignant moment. No man could have been unaffected by the girl's tragic story. Mason paced to and fro, then halted behind the table.

"Boss, that's not all," interposed Reed triumphantly. "Down at Halsey, Hildrith showed his color—and what meant most to him. Brittenham was there, as I've told you. And *he* was on to us. I saw the jig was up. I told Hildrith. I put it up to him. To declare himself. Every man there had waked up to the fact that we were horse thieves. I asked Hildrith to make his stand—for or against us. He failed us, boss."

"Reed, that was a queer thing for you to insist on," declared Mason, in stern doubt. "Hildrith's cue was the same as mine. Respectability. Could you expect him to betray himself there—before all Halsey and his sweetheart, too?"

"I knew he wouldn't. But I meant it."

"You wanted to show him up, before them all, especially her?"

"I certainly did."

"Well, you're low-down yourself, Reed, when it comes to one you hate."

"All's fair in love and war," replied the other with a flippant laugh.

The chief turned to Hildrith. "I'm not concerned with the bad blood between you and Reed. But—is he lying?"

"No. But down at Halsey I didn't understand he meant me to give myself away," replied Hildrith, with the calmness of bitter resignation. He had played a great game, for a great stake, and he had lost. Friendship, loyalty, treachery, were nothing compared to his love for this girl.

"Would you have done so if you had understood Reed?"

"No. Why should I? There was no disloyalty in that. If I'd guessed that, I'd have shot him."

"You didn't think quick and right. That'd have been your game. Too late, Hildrith. I've a hunch it's too late for all of us. . . . You meant to marry Miss Watrous if she'd have you?"

"Why ask that?"

"Well, it was unnecessary. . . . And you really let this Brittenham sacrifice himself for you?"

"Yes, I'd have sacrificed anyone—my own brother!"

"I see. That was dirty, Leale. . . . But after all these things, don't . . . You've been a faithful pard for many years. God knows a woman . . ."

"Boss, he betrayed *you*," interrupted Reed stridently. "All the rest doesn't count. He split with you. He absolutely was not going to leave the country with you."

"I get that—hard as it is to believe," rasped Mason, and he took up the big gun from the table and deliberately cocked it.

Edith cried out low and falteringly. "Oh—don't kill him! If it was for me—spare him."

Reed let out that sardonic laugh. "Bah! He'll deny—he'll lie with his last breath."

"That wouldn't save you, Leale—but—" Mason halted, the dark embodiment of honor among thieves.

"Hell, I deny nothing!" rang out Hildrith, with something grand in his defiance. "It's all true. I broke over the girl. I was through with you, Mason—you and your raids, you and your lousy sneak here—you and your low-down . . ."

The leveled gun boomed to cut short Hildrith's wild denunciation. Shot through the heart, he swayed a second, his distorted visage fixing, and then, with a single explosion of gasping breath, he fell backward through the door.

• 4 •

A HEAVY CLOUD OF SMOKE OBSCURED DALE'S SIGHT OF the center of the cabin. As he leaned there near the window, strung like a quivering wire, he heard the thump of Mason's gun on the table. It made the gold coins jingle in their sacks. The thud of boots and hoarse shouts arose on the far side of the cabin. Then the smoke drifted away to expose Mason hunched back against the table, peering through the door into the blackness. Reed knelt on the floor where Edith had sunk in a faint.

Other members of the gang arrived outside the cabin. "Hyar! It's Hildrith. Reckon the boss croaked him."

"Mebbe Reed did it. He sure was hankerin' to."

"How air you, chief?" called a third man, presenting a swarthy face in the lamplight.

"I'm—all right," replied Mason huskily. "Hildrith betrayed us. I bored him. . . . Drag him away. . . . You can divide what you find on him."

"Hey, I'm in on that," called Reed, as the swarthy man backed away from the door. "Lay hold, fellers."

Slow, labored footfalls died away. Mason opened his gun to eject the discharged shell and to replace it with one from his belt.

"She keeled over," said Reed as he lifted the girl's head.

"So I see. . . . Sudden and raw for a tenderfoot. I'm damn glad she hated him. . . . Did you see him feeling for his gun?"

"No. It's just as well I took that away from him on the way up. Nothing yellow about Hildrith at the finish."

"Queer what a woman can do to a man! Reed, haven't you lost your head over this one?"

"Hell yes!" exploded the other.

"Better turn her loose. She'll handicap you. This hole will be swarming with posses tomorrow."

"You're sloping tonight?"

"I am. How many horses did you sell?"

"Eighty odd. None under a hundred dollars. And we drove back the best."

"Keep it. Pay your outfit. We're square. My advice is let this Watrous girl go, and make tracks away from here."

"Thanks. . . . But I won't leave any tracks," returned Reed constrainedly. "She's coming too."

"Pack her out of here. . . . Reed, I wouldn't be in your boots for a million."

"And just why, boss?"

"Women always were your weakness. Your only one. You'll hang on to the Watrous girl."

"You bet your life I will."

"Don't bet my life on it. You're gambling your own. And you'll lose it."

Reed picked up the reviving Edith and took her through the door, turning sidewise to keep from striking her head. Dale's last glimpse of his gloating expression, as he gazed down into her face, nerved him to instant and reckless action. Reed had turned to the left outside the door, which gave Dale the impression that he did not intend to carry the girl toward the campfires.

Nalook touched Dale and silently indicated that he would go around to his end of the cabin. Dale turned to the left. At the corner he waited to peer out. He saw a dark form cross the campfire light. Reed! He was turning away from his comrades, now engaged in a heated hubbub, no doubt over money and valuables they had found on Hildrith.

Dale had to fight his overwhelming eagerness. He stole out to follow Reed. The man made directly for the shack that Dale and Nalook had passed on their stalk to the cabin. Dale did not stop to see if the Indian followed, though he expected him to do so. Dale held himself to an absolutely noiseless stealth. The deep grass made that possible.

Edith let out a faint cry, scarcely audible. It seemed to loose springs of fire in Dale's muscles. He glided on, gaining upon the outlaw with his burden. They drew away from the vicinity of the campfires. Soon Dale grew sufficiently accustomed to the starlight to keep track of Reed. The girl was speaking incoherently. Dale would rather have had her still unconscious. She might scream and draw Reed's comrades in that direction.

Under the trees, between the bunches of scrub oak, Reed hurried. His panting breath grew quite audible. Edith was no slight burden, especially as she had begun to struggle in his arms.

"Where? . . . Who? Let me down," she cried, but weakly.

"Shut up, or I'll bat you one," he panted.

The low shack loomed up blacker than the shadows. A horse, tethered in the gloom, snorted at Reed's approach. Dale, now only a few paces behind the outlaw, gathered all his forces for a spring.

"Let me go. . . . Let me go. . . . I'll scream—"

"Shut up, I tell you. If you scream I'll choke you. If you fight, I'll beat you."

"But Reed—for God's sake! . . . You're not drunk. You must be mad—if you mean . . ."

"Girl, I didn't know what—I meant—when I grabbed you down there," he panted, passionately. "But now I know. . . . I'm taking you away—Edith Watrous—out of Montana. . . . But tonight, by heaven! . . ."

Dale closed in swiftly and silently. With relentless strength he crushed a strangling hold around Reed's neck. The man snorted as his head went back. The girl dropped with a sudden gasp. Then Dale, the fingers of his left hand buried in Reed's throat, released his right hand to grasp his gun. He did not dare to shoot, but he swung the weapon to try to stun Reed. He succeeded in landing only a glancing blow.

"Aaggh!" gasped Reed, and for an instant his body appeared to sink.

Dale tried to strike again. Because of Reed's sudden grip on his arm he could not exert enough power. The gun stuck. Dale felt it catch in the man's coat. Reed let out a strangled yell, which Dale succeeded in choking off again.

Suddenly the outlaw let go Dale's right hand and reached for his gun. He got to it, but could not draw, due to Dale's constricting arm. Dale pressed with all his might. They staggered, swayed, bound together as with bands of steel. Dale saw that if his hold loosened on either Reed's throat or gun hand, the issue would be terribly perilous. Reed was the larger and more powerful, though now at a disadvantage. Dale hung on like the grim death he meant to mete out to this man.

Suddenly, with a tremendous surge Reed broke Dale's hold and bent him back. Then Dale saw he would be forced to shoot. But even as he struggled with the gun, Reed, quick as a cat, intercepted it, and with irresistible strength turned the weapon away while he drew his own. Dale was swift to grasp that with his left hand. A terrific struggle ensued, during which the grim and silent combatants both lost hold of their guns.

Reed succeeded in drawing a knife, which he swung aloft. Dale caught his wrist and jerked down on it with such tremendous force that he caused the outlaw to stab himself in the side. Then Dale grappled him round the waist, pinning both arms to Reed's sides, so that he was unable to withdraw the knife. Not only that, but soon Dale's inexorable pressure sank the blade in to the hilt. A horrible panting sound escaped Reed's lips.

Any moment Nalook might come to end this desperate struggle. The knife stuck in Reed's side, clear to the hilt. Dale had the thought that he must hold on until Reed collapsed. Then he would have to run with Edith and try to get up the trail. He could not hope to find the horses in that gloomy shadow.

Reed grew stronger in his frenzy. He whirled so irresistibly that he partly broke Dale's hold. They plunged down, with Dale on the top and Reed under him. Dale had his wind almost shut off. Another moment . . . But Reed rolled like a bear. Dale, now underneath, wound his left arm around Reed. Over and over they rolled, against the cabin, back against a tree, and then over a bank. The shock broke both Dale's holds. Reed essayed to yell, but only a hoarse sound came forth. Suddenly he had weakened. Dale beat at him with his right fist. Then he reached for the knife in Reed's side, found the hilt and wrenched so terrifically that he cracked Reed's ribs. The man suddenly relaxed. Dale tore the knife out and buried it in Reed's breast.

That ended the fight. Reed sank shudderingly into a limp state. Dale slowly got up, drawing the knife with him. He had sustained no injury that he could ascertain at the moment. He was wet with sweat or blood, probably both. He slipped the knife in his belt, and untied his scarf to wipe his hands and face. Then he climbed up the bank, expecting to see Edith's white blouse in the darkness.

But he did not see it. Nor was Nalook there. He called low. No answer! He began to search around on the ground. He found his gun. Then he went into the shack. Edith was gone and Nalook had not come. Possibly he might have come while the fight was going on down over the bank and, seeing the chance to save Edith, had made off with her to the horses.

Dale listened. The crickets were in loud voice. He could see the campfire, and heard nothing except the thud of hoofs. They seemed fairly close. He retraced his steps back to the shack. Reed's horse was gone. Dale strove for control over his whirling thoughts. He feared that Edith, in her terror, had run off at random, to be captured again by some of the outlaws. After a moment's consideration, he dismissed that as untenable. She had fled, unquestionably, but without a cry, which augured well. Dale searched the black rim for the notch that marked the trail. Then he set off.

Reaching the belt of brush under the rim he followed it until he came to an opening he thought he recognized. A stamp of hoofs electrified him. He hurried toward it and presently emerged into a glade less gloomy. First his keen sight distinguished Edith's white blouse. She was either sitting or lying on the ground. Then he saw the horses. As he hurried forward, Nalook met him.

"Nalook! Is she all right?" he whispered eagerly.

"All same okay. No hurt."

"What'd you do?"

"Me foller. See girl run. Me ketch."

"Go back to that shack and search Reed. He must have a lot of money on him. . . . We rolled over a bank."

"Ugh!" The Indian glided away.

Dale went on to find Edith sitting propped against a stone. He could not distinguish her features but her posture was eloquent of spent force.

"Edith," he called gently.

"Oh—Dale! . . . Are you—?"

"I'm all right," he replied hastily.

"You—killed him?"

"Of course. I had to. Are you hurt?"

"Only bruised. That ride! . . . Then he handled me—Oh, the brute! I'm glad you killed . . . I saw you bend him back—hit him. I knew you. But it was awful. . . . And seeing Leale murdered—so suddenly—right before my eyes—that was worse."

"Put that all out of your mind. . . . Let me help you up. We can't stay here long. Your hands are like ice," he whispered as he got her up.

"I'm freezing—to death," she replied. "This thin waist. I left my coat in the buckboard."

"Here. Slip into mine." Dale helped her into his coat, and then began to rub her cold hands between his.

"Dale, I wasn't afraid of Reed—at first. I scorned him. I saw how his men liked that. I kept telling him that you would kill him for this outrage to me. That if *you* didn't Dad would hang him. But there in Mason's cabin—there I realized my danger. . . . You must have been close."

"Yes. Nalook and I watched between the logs. I saw it all. But I tell you to forget it."

"Oh, will I ever? . . . Dale, you saved me from God only knows what," she whispered, and putting her arms around his neck, she leaned upon his breast, and looked up. Out of her pale face great midnight eyes that reflected the starlight transfixed him with their mystery and passion. "You liar! You fool!" she went on, her soft voice belying the hard words. "You poor misguided man! To dishonor your name for Hildrith's sake! To tell Stafford he was right! To let Dad hear you say you were a horse thief! . . . Oh! I shall never forgive you!"

"My dear. I did it—for Leale—and perhaps more for your sake," replied Dale unsteadily. "I thought you loved him. That was his chance to reform. He would have done it, too, if—"

"I don't care what he would have done. I imagined I loved him. But I didn't. I was a vain, silly, headstrong girl. And I was influenced. I don't believe I ever could have married him—after you brought back my horses. I didn't realize then. But when I kissed you—Oh, Dale! Something tore through my heart. I know now. It was love. Even then! . . . Oh, I needed this horrible experience. It has awakened me. . . . Oh, Dale, if I loved you then, what do you think it is now?"

"I can't think—dearest," whispered Dale huskily, as he drew her closer, and bent over her to lay his face against her hair. "Only, if you're not out of your mind, I'm the luckiest man thet ever breathed."

"Dale, I'm distraught, yes, and my heart is bursting. But I know I love you . . . love you—love you! Oh, with all my mind and soul."

Dale heard in a tumultuous exaltation, and he stood holding her with a intensely vivid sense of the place and moment. The ragged rim loomed above them, dark and forbidding, as if to warn; the incessant chirp of crickets, the murmur of running water, the rustle of the wind in the brush, proved that he was alive and awake, living the most poignant moment of his life.

Then Nalook glided silently into the glade. Dale released Edith, and stepped back to meet the Indian. Nalook thrust into his hands a heavy bundle tied up in a scarf.

"Me keep gun," he said, and bent over his saddle.

"What'll we do, Nalook?" asked Dale.

"Me stay—watch trail. You take girl Halsey."

"Dale, I couldn't ride it. I'm exhausted. I can hardly stand," interposed Edith.

"Reckon I'd get lost in the dark," returned Dale thoughtfully. "I've got a better plan. There's a homesteader in this valley. Man named Rogers. I knew him over in the mountains. An' I ran across his cabin a day or so ago. It's not far. I'll take you there. Then tomorrow I'll go with you to Bannock, or send you with him."

"Send me!"

"Yes. I've got to be here. Strickland agreed to send a posse after me in half an hour—an' later a big outfit of cowboys."

"But you've rescued me. Need you stay? Nalook can guide these men."

"I reckon I want to help clean out these horse thieves."

"Bayne is on *your* trail with a posse."

"Probably he's with Stafford's outfit."

"That won't clear you of Stafford's accusation."

"No. But Strickland an' his outfit will clear me. I must be here when thet fight comes off. *If* it comes. You heard Mason say he was leavin' to-night. I reckon they'll all get out pronto."

"Dale! You—you might get shot—or even . . . Oh, these are wicked, hard men!" exclaimed Edith, as she fastened persuasive hands on his coatless arms.

"Thet's the chance I have to run to clear my name, Edith," he rejoined gravely.

"You took a fearful chance with Reed."

"Yes. But he had you in his power."

"My life and more were at stake then," she said earnestly. "It's still my love and my happiness."

"Edith, I'll have Nalook beside me an' we'll fight like Indians. I swear I'll come out of it alive."

"Then—go ahead—anyway. . . ." she whispered almost inaudibly, and let her nerveless hands drop from him.

"Nalook, you watch the trail," ordered Dale. "Stop any man climbing out. When Strickland's posse comes, hold them till the cowboys get here. If I hear shots this way, I'll come pronto."

The Indian grunted and, taking up his rifle, stole away. Dale untied and led his horse up to where his saddle lay. Soon he had him saddled and bri-dled. Then he put on his spurs, which the Indian had remembered to get.

"Come on," said Dale, reaching for Edith. When he lifted her, it came home to him why Reed had not found it easy to carry her.

"That's comfortable, if I can stay on," she said, settling herself.

"Hoofs, old boy," whispered Dale to his horse. "No actin' up. This'll be the most precious load you ever carried."

Then Dale, rifle in hand, took the bridle and led the horse out into the open. The lake gleamed like a black starlit mirror. Turning to the right, Dale slowly chose the ground and walked a hundred steps or more before he halted to listen. He went on and soon crossed the trail. Beyond that he breathed easier, and did not stop again until he had half circled the lake. He saw lights across the water up among the trees, but heard no alarming sound.

"How're you ridin'?" he whispered to Edith.

"I can stick on if it's not too far."

"Half a mile more."

As he proceeded, less fearful of being heard, he began to calculate about where he should look for Rogers's canyon. He had carefully marked it almost halfway between the two lakes and directly across from the highest point of the rim. When Dale got abreast of this he headed to the right, and was soon under the west wall. Then, despite the timber on the rim and the shadowed background, he located a gap which he made certain marked the canyon.

But he could not find any trail leading into it. Therefore he began to work a cautious way through the thickets. The gurgle and splash of running water guided him. It was so pitch black that he had to feel his way. The watercourse turned out to be rocky and he abandoned that. When he began to fear he was headed wrong, a dark tunnel led him out into the open canyon. He went on and turned a corner to catch the gleam of a light. Then he rejoiced at his good fortune. In a few minutes more he arrived at the cabin. The door was open. Dale heard voices.

"Hey, Rogers, are you home?" he called.

An exclamation and thud of bootless feet attested to the homesteader's presence. The next instant he appeared in the door.

"Who's thar?"

"Brittenham," replied Dale, and lifting Edith off the saddle, he carried her up on the porch into the light. Rogers came out in amazement. His wife cried from the door, "For land's sake!"

"Wal, a gurl! Aw, don't say she's hurt," burst out the homesteader.

"You bet it's a girl. An' thank heaven she's sound! Jim Watrous's daughter, Rogers. She was kidnapped by Reed at the Halsey horse sale. Thet happened this afternoon. I just got her back. Now. Mrs. Rogers, will you take her in for tonight? Hide her someplace."

"That I will. She can sleep in the loft. . . . Come in, my dear child. You're white as a sheet."

"Thank you. I've had enough to make me green," replied Edith, limping into the cabin.

Dale led Rogers out of earshot. "Hell will bust loose here about tomorrow," he said, and briefly told about the several posses en route for the horse thieves' stronghold, and the events relating to the capture and rescue of Edith.

"By gad! Thet's all good," ejaculated the homesteader. "But it's not so good—all of us hyar if they have a big fight."

"Maybe the gang will slope. Mason is leavin'. I heard him tell Reed. An' Reed meant to take the girl. I don't know about the rest of them."

"Wal, these fellers ain't likely to rustle in the dark. They've been too secure. An' they figger they can't be surprised at night."

"If Mason leaves by the lower trail, he'll get shot. My Indian pard is watchin' there."

"Gosh, I hope he tries it."

"Mason had his table loaded with bags of coin an' stacks of bills. We sure ought to get thet an' pay back the people he's robbed."

"It's a good bet Mason won't take the upper trail. . . . Brittenham, you look fagged. Better have some grub an' drink. An' sleep a little."

"Sure. But I'm a bloody mess, an' don't want

the women to see me. Fetch me somethin' out here."

Later Dale and Rogers walked down to the valley. They did not see any lights or hear any sounds. Both ends of the gorge, where the trails led up, were dark and silent. They returned, and Dale lay down on the porch on some sheepskins. He did not expect to sleep. His mind was too full. Only the imminence of a battle could have kept his mind off the wondrous and incomprehensible fact of Edith's avowal. After pondering over the facts and probabilities Dale decided a fight was inevitable. Mason and Reed had both impressed him as men at the end of their ropes. The others would, no doubt, leave, though not so hurriedly, and most probably would be met on the way out.

Long after Rogers's cabin was dark and its inmates wrapped in slumber, Dale lay awake, listening, thinking, revolving plans to get Edith safely away and still not seem to shirk his share of the fight. But at last, worn out by strenuous activity and undue call on his emotions, Dale fell asleep.

A step on the porch aroused him. It was broad daylight. Rogers was coming in with an armload of firewood.

"All serene, Brittenham," he said, with satisfaction.

"Good. I'll wash an' slip down to get a look at the valley."

"Wal, I'd say if these outfits of cowboys was on hand, they'd be down long ago."

"Me too." Dale did not go clear out into the gateway of the valley. He climbed to a ruddy eminence and surveyed the gorge from the lookout. Sweeping the gray-green valley with eager gaze, he failed to see a moving object. Both upper and lower ends of the gorge appeared as vacant as they were silent. But at length he quickened sharply to columns of blue smoke rising above the timber up from the lower lake. He watched for a good hour. The sun rose over the gap at the east rim. Concluding that posses and cowboys had yet to arrive, Dale descended the bluff and retraced his steps toward the cabin.

He considered sending Edith out in charge of Rogers, to conduct her as far as Bannock. This idea he at once conveyed to Rogers.

"Don't think much of it," returned the homesteader forcibly. "Better hide her an' my family in a cave. I know where they'll be safe until this fracas is over."

"Well! I reckon thet is better."

"Come in an' eat. Then we'll go scoutin'. An' if we see any riders, we'll rustle back to hide the women an' kids."

Dale had about finished a substantial breakfast when he thought he heard a horse neigh somewhere at a distance. He ran out on the porch and was suddenly shocked to a standstill. Scarcely ten paces out stood a man with leveled rifle.

"Hands up, Britt," he ordered, with a hissing breath. Two other men, just behind him, leaped forward to present guns, and one of them yelled, "Yar he is, Bayne."

"Rustle! Up with 'em!"

Then Dale, realizing the cold bitter fact of an unlooked-for situation, shot up his arms just as Rogers came stamping out.

"What the hell?" Who . . ."

Six or eight more men, guns in hands, appeared at the right, led by the red-faced sheriff of Salmon. He appeared to be bursting with importance and vicious triumph. Dale surveyed the advancing group, among whom he recognized old enemies, and then his gaze flashed back to the first man with the leveled rifle. This was none other than

Pickens, a crooked young horse trader who had all the reason in the world to gloat over rounding up Dale in this way.

"Guess I didn't have a hunch up thar, fellers, when we crossed this trail," declared Bayne in loud voice. "Guess I didn't measure his hoss tracks down at Watrous's for nothin'!"

"Bayne, you got the drop," spoke up Dale coolly, "and I'm not fool enough to draw in the face of thet."

"You did draw on me once, though, didn't you?"

"Yes."

"An' you told Stafford he was right, didn't you?"

"Yes, but . . ."

"No buts. You admitted you was a hoss thief, didn't you?"

"Rogers here can explain thet, if you won't listen to me."

"Wal, Brittenham, your homesteadin' pard can explain thet after we hang you!"

Rogers stalked off the porch in the very face of the menacing guns and confronted Bayne in angry expostulation.

"See here, Mister Bayne, you're on the wrong track."

"We want no advice from you," shouted Bayne. "An' you'd better look out or we'll give you the same dose."

"Boss, he's shore one of this hoss-thief gang," spoke up a lean, weathered member of the posse.

"My name's Rogers. I'm a homesteader. I have a wife an' two children. There are men in Bannock who'll vouch for my honesty," protested Rogers.

"Reckon so. But they ain't here. You stay out of this. . . . Hold him up, men."

Two of them prodded the homesteader with cocked rifles, a reckless and brutal act that would have made the bravest man turn gray. Rogers put up shaking hands.

"Friend Rogers, don't interfere," warned Dale, who had grasped the deadly nature of Bayne's procedure. The sheriff believed Dale was one of the mysterious band of thieves that had been harassing the ranchers of Salmon River Valley for a long time. It had galled him, no doubt, to fail to bring a single thief to justice. Added to that was an animosity toward Dale and a mean leaning to exercise his office. He wanted no trial. He would brook no opposition. Dale stood there a self-confessed criminal.

"Rope Brittenham," ordered Bayne. "Tie his hands behind his back. Bore him if he as much as winks."

Two of the posse dragged Dale off the porch, and in a moment had bound him securely. Then Dale realized too late that he should have leaped while he was free to snatch a gun from one of his captors, and fought it out. He had not taken seriously Bayne's threat to hang him. But he saw now that unless a miracle came to pass, he was doomed. The thought was so appalling that it clamped him momentarily in an icy terror. Edith was at the back of the emotion. He had faced death before without flinching, but to be hanged while Edith was there, possibly a witness—that would be too horrible. Yet he read it in the hard visages of Bayne and his men. By a tremendous effort he succeeded in getting hold of himself.

"Bayne, this job is not law," he expostulated. "It's revenge. When my innocence is proved, you'll be in a tight fix."

"Innocence! Hell, man, didn't you confess your guilt?" ejaculated Bayne. "Stafford heard you, same as Watrous an' his friends."

"All the same, thet was a lie."

"Aw, it was? My Gawd, man, but you take chances with your life! An' what'd you lie for?"

"I lied for Edith Watrous."

Bayne stared incredulously and then he guffawed. He turned to his men.

"Reckon we better shet off his wind. The man's plumb loco."

From behind Dale a noose, thrown by a lanky cowboy, sailed and widened to encircle his head, and to be drawn tight. The hard knot came just under Dale's chin and shut off the hoarse cry that formed involuntarily.

"Over thet limb, feller," called out Bayne briskly, pointing to a spreading branch of piñon tree some few yards farther out. Dale was dragged under it. The loose end of the rope was thrown over the branch, to fall into eager hands.

"Dirty bizness, Bayne, you . . . !" shouted Rogers, shaken by horror and wrath. "So help me Gawd, you'll rue it!"

Bayne leered malignantly, plainly in the grip of passion too strong for reason.

"Thar's five thousand dollars' reward wrapped up in this wild-hoss hunter's hide an' I ain't takin' any chance of losin' it."

Dale forced a strangled utterance. "Bayne—I'll double thet—if you'll arrest me . . . give . . . fair trial."

"Haw! Haw! Haw! Wal, listen to our ragged hoss thief talk big money."

"Boss, he ain't got two bits. . . . We're wastin' time."

"Swing him fellers!"

Four or five men stretched the rope and had lifted Dale to his toes when a piercing shriek from the cabin startled them so violently that they let him down again. Edith Watrous came flying out, half dressed, her hair down, her face blanched.

Her white blouse fluttered in her hand as she ran bare-footed across the grass.

"Merciful heaven! Dale! That rope!" she screamed, and as the shock of realization came, she dropped her blouse to the ground and stood stricken before the staring men, her bare round arms and lovely shoulders shining white in the sunlight. Her eyes darkened, dilated, enlarged as her consciousness grasped the significance here, and then fixed in terror.

Dale's ghastly sense of death faded. This girl would save him. A dozen Baynes could not contend with Edith Watrous, once she was roused.

"Edith, they were about—to hang me."

"Hang you?" she cried, suddenly galvanized. "These men? . . . Bayne?"

Leaping red blood burned out the pallor of her face. It swept away in a wave, leaving her whiter than before, and with eyes like coals of living fire.

"Miss—Watrous. What you—doin' here?" queried Bayne, halting, confused by this apparition.

"I'm here—not quite too late," she replied, as if to herself, and a ring of certainty in her voice followed hard on the tremulous evidence of her thought.

"Kinda queer—meetin' you up here in this outlaw den," went on Bayne with a nervous cough.

"Bayne . . . I remember," she said ponderingly, ignoring his statement. "The gossip linking Dale's name with this horse-thief outfit. . . . Stafford! . . . Your intent to arrest Dale! . . . His drawing on you! His strange acceptance of Stafford's accusation!"

"Nothin' strange about thet, Miss," rejoined Bayne brusquely. "Brittenham was caught in a trap. An' like a wolf he bit back."

"That confession had to do with me, Mister Bayne," she retorted.

"So he said. But I ain't disregardin' same."

"You are not arresting him," she asserted swiftly.

"Nope, I ain't."

"But didn't you let him explain?" she asked.

"I didn't want no cock-an'-bull explainin' from him or this doubtful pard of his here, Rogers. . . . I'll just hang Brittenham an' let Rogers talk afterwards. Reckon he'll not have much to say then."

"So that's your plan, you miserable thick-headed skunk of a sheriff?" she exclaimed in lashing scorn. She swept her flaming eyes from Bayne to his posse, all of whom appeared uneasy over this interruption. "Pickens! . . . Hall! . . . Jason Pike! And some more hard nuts from Salmon. Why, if you were honest yourself, you'd arrest them. My father could put Pickens in jail. . . . Bayne, your crew of a posse reflects suspiciously on you."

"Wal, I ain't carin' for what you think. It's plain to me you've took powerful with this hoss thief an' I reckon thet reflects suspicious on you, Miss," rejoined Bayne, galled to recrimination.

A scarlet blush wiped out the whiteness of Edith's neck and face. She burned with shame and fury. That seemed to remind her of herself, of her half-dressed state, and she bent to pick up her blouse. When she rose to slip her arms through the garment she was pale again. She forgot to button it.

"You dare not hang Brittenham."

"Wal, lady, I just do," he declared, but he was weakening somehow.

"You shall not!"

"Better go indoors, Miss. It ain't pleasant to see a man hang an' kick an' swell an' grow black in the face."

Bayne had no conception of the passion and courage of a woman. He blundered into the very speeches that made Edith a lioness.

"Take that rope off his neck," she commanded, as a queen might have to slaves.

The members of the posse shifted from one foot to the other, and betrayed that they would have looked to their leader had they been able to remove their fascinated gaze from this girl. Pickens, the nearest to her, moved back a step, holding his rifle muzzle up. The freckles stood out awkwardly on his dirty white face.

"Give me that rifle," she cried hotly, and she leaped to snatch at it. Pickens held on, his visage a study in consternation and alarm. Edith let go with one hand and struck him a staggering blow with her fist. Then she fought him for the weapon. *Bang!* It belched fire and smoke up into the tree. She jerked it away from him and, leaping back, she worked the lever with a swift precision that proved her familiarity with firearms. Without aiming she shot at Pickens's feet. Dale saw the bullet strike up dust between them. Pickens leaped with a wild yell and fled.

Edith whirled upon Bayne. She was magnificent in her rage. Such a thing as fear of these men was as far from her as if she had never experienced such an emotion. Again she worked the action of the rifle. She held it low at Bayne and pulled the trigger. *Bang!* That bullet sped between his legs, and burned the left one, which flinched as the man called, "Hyar! Stop thet, you fool woman. You'll kill somebody!"

"Bayne, I'll kill *you*, if you try to hang Brittenham," she replied, her voice ringing high-keyed but level and cold. "Take that noose off his neck!"

The frightened sheriff made haste to comply.

"Now untie him!"

"Help me hyar—somebody," snarled Bayne, turning Dale around to tear at the rope. "My Gawd, what's this range comin' to when wild women bust loose! ——— the luck! We can't shoot her! We can't rope Jim Watrous's girl!"

"Boss, I reckon it may be jist as well," replied the lean gray man who was helping him, "cause it wasn't regular."

"You men! Put away your guns," ordered Edith. "I wouldn't hesitate to shoot any one of you.... Now listen, all of you. Brittenham is no horse thief. He is a man who sacrificed his name—his honor for his friend—and because he thought I loved that friend. Leale Hildrith! He was the treacherous spy—the go-between—the liar who deceived my father and me. Dale took his guilt. I never believed it. I followed Dale to Halsey. Hildrith followed me. There we found Ed Reed and his outfit selling Watrous horses. I recognized my own horse, Dick, and I accused Reed. He betrayed Hildrith right there and kidnapped us both, and rode to this hole.... We got here last night. Reed took me before Bill Mason. Big Bill, who is the leader of this band. They sent for Hildrith. And Mason shot him. Reed made off with me, intending to leave. But Dale had trailed us, and he killed Reed. Then he fetched me here to this cabin.... You have my word. I swear this is the truth."

"Wal, I'll be ...!" ejaculated Bayne, who had grown so obsessed by Edith's story that he had forgotten to untie Dale.

"Boss! Hosses comin' hell-bent!" shouted one of Bayne's men, running in.

"Whar?"

A ringing trample of swift hoofs on the hard trail drowned further shouts. Dale saw a line of riders sweep round the corner and race right down upon the cabin. They began to shoot into

Bayne's posse. There were six riders, all shooting as hard as they were riding, and some of them had two guns leveled. Hoarse yells rose about the banging volley of shots. The horsemen sped on past, still shooting. Bullets thudded into the cabin. The riders vanished in a cloud of dust and the clatter of hoofs died away.

Dale frantically unwound the rope which Bayne had suddenly let go at the onslaught of the riders. Freeing himself, Dale leaped to Edith, who had dropped the rifle and stood unsteadily, her eyes wild.

"Did they—hit you?" gasped Dale, seizing her.

"No, but look!"

Rogers rushed up to join them, holding a hand to a bloody shoulder. "Some of Mason's outfit," he boomed, and he gazed around with rolling eyes. Pickens lay dead, his bloody head against the tree. Bayne had been shot through the middle. A spreading splotch of red on his shirt under his clutching hands attested to a mortal wound. Three other men lay either groaning or cursing. That left four apparently unscratched, only one of whom, a lean oldish man, showed any inclination to help his comrades.

"Lemme see how bad you're hit," he was growling over one of them.

"Aw, it ain't bad, but it hurts like hell."

"Edith, come, I'll take you in," said Dale, putting his arm around the weakening girl.

"Britt, I've a better idee," put in Rogers. "I'll take her an' my family to the cave where they'll be safe."

"Good! Thet outfit must have been chased."

"We'd have heard shots. I reckon they were rustlin' away and jest piled into us."

The two reached the cabin, where Dale said,

"Brace up, Edith. It sure was tough. It'll be all right now."

"Oh, I'm sick," she whispered, as she leaned against him.

Rogers went in, calling to his wife. Dale heard him rummaging around. Soon he appeared in the door and handed a tin box and a bundle of linen to Dale.

"Those hombres out there can take care of their own wounded." Dale pressed Edith's limp hand and begged earnestly, "Don't weaken now, dear. Good Lord, how wonderful an' terrible you were! . . . Edith, I'll bear a charmed life after this. . . . Go with Rogers. An' don't worry, darlin'. . . . The Mason gang is on the run, thet's sure."

"I'll be all right," she replied with a pale smile. "Go—do what's best—but don't stay long away from me."

Hurrying out, Dale found all save one of the wounded on their feet.

"Wal, thet's decent of you," said the lean, hawk-faced man, as he received the bandages and medicine from Dale. "Bayne jist croaked an' he can stay croaked right there for all I care. I'm sorry he made the mistake takin' you for a hoss thief."

"He paid for it," rejoined Dale grimly. "You must bury him and Pickens. I'll fetch you some tools. But move them away from here."

Dale searched around until he found a spade and mattock, which he brought back. Meanwhile the spokesman of Bayne's posse and Jason Pike had about concluded a hasty binding of the injured men.

"Brittenham, we come down this trail from Bannock. Are there any other ways to get in an' out of this hole?"

"Look here," replied Dale, and squatted down to draw an oval in the dust. "This represents the valley. It runs almost directly north an' south. There's a trail at each end. This trail of Rogers's heads out of there almost due west, an' leads to Bannock. There might be, an' very probably is, another trail on the east side, perhaps back of Mason's camp. But Nalook didn't tell me there was."

"Thet outfit who rid by here to smoke us up—they must have been chased or at least scared."

"Chased, I figure that, though no cowboys appear to be comin' along. You know Stafford an' Watrous were sendin' a big outfit of cowboys up from Salmon. They'll come down the south trail. An' I'm responsible for two more, raised by a rancher named Strickland over at Halsey. They are due an' they'll come in at the lower end of the hole. The north end."

"Wal, I'd like to be in on the round-up. What say, Jason?"

"Hell, yes, but Tom, you'd better send Jerry an' hike out with our cripples. They'd just handicap us."

"Reckon so. Now let's rustle to put these stiffs under the sod an' the dew. Strip them of valuables. Funny about Bayne. He was sure rarin' to spend that five thousand Stafford offered for Brittenham alive or dead."

"Bayne had some faults. He was some previous on this job. . . . Hyar, fellers, give us a hand."

"I'll rustle my horse," said Dale, and strode off. He had left Hoofs to graze at will, but the sturdy bay was nowhere in sight. Finally Dale found him in Rogers's corral with two other horses. He led Hoofs back to the cabin, and was saddling him when he saw Rogers crossing the brook into the open. Evidently he had taken the women and children somewhere in that direction. Dale's keen eye approved of the dense thicket of brush and trees leading up to a great wall of cliffs and caverns and splintered sections. They would be safely hidden in there.

Then Dale bethought himself of his gun, which Pickens had taken from him. He found it under the tree with the weapons, belts, and spurs of the slain men. Dale took up the carbine that Pickens had held, and which Edith had wrenched out of his hands. He decided he would like to keep it, and carried it to the cabin.

Tom and Pike, with the third man, returned from their gruesome task somewhere below. The next move was to send the four cripples, one of whom lurched in his saddle, up the trail to Bannock with their escort.

When Dale turned from the dubious gaze after them, he sighted Nalook riding up from the valley. The Indian appeared to be approaching warily. Dale hallooed and strode out to meet him.

The Indian pointed with dark hand at the hoof tracks in the trail.

"Me come slow—look see."

"Nalook, those tracks were made by six of Mason's outfit who rode through, hell-bent for election."

"Me hear shots."

"They killed Bayne an' one of his posse, an' crippled four more."

"Ugh! Bayne jail Injun no more!" Nalook ejaculated with satisfaction.

"I should smile not. But, Nalook, what's doin' down in the hole?"

"Ten paleface, three my people come sunup. No cowboy."

"Well! Thet's odd. Strickland guaranteed a big outfit. I wonder. . . . No sign of Stafford's cowboys on the other trail?"

"Me look long, no come."

"Where's thet outfit from Halsey?"

The Indian indicated by gesture that he had detained these men at the rim.

"You watch trail all night?"

Nalook nodded, and his inscrutable eyes directed Dale's to the back of his saddle. A dark coat of heavy material, and evidently covering a bundle, had been bound behind the cantle. Dale put a curious hand on the coat. He felt something hard inside, and that caused him to note how securely and tightly the coat had been tied on. Suddenly a dark red spot gave him a shock. Blood! He touched it to find it a smear glazed over and dry. Dale looked into the bronzed visage and somber eyes of the Indian with a cold sense of certainty.

"Mason?"

The Indian nodded. "Me watch long. Big Bill he come. Two paleface foller. Top trail. Me watch. Big powwow. They want gold. Mason no give. Cuss like hell! They shoot. Me kill um."

"Nalook, you just beat hell!" ejaculated Dale, at once thrilled and overcome at the singular way things were working out. He had not forgotten the sacks of gold and pile of greenbacks on Mason's table. To let the robber chief make off with that had been no easy surrender.

"Me beat hoss thief," replied the Indian, taking Dale literally. "Big Bill no good. He take Palouse girl away."

"Aha! So thet's why you've been so soft and gentle with these horse thieves. . . . Nalook, I don't want anyone, not even Rogers, to see this coat an' what's in it."

"Me savvy. Where hide?"

"Go to the barn. Hide it in the loft under the hay."

Nalook rode on by the cabin. Dale sat down on the porch to wait for his return and the others. He found himself trembling with the significance of the moment. He had possession of a large amount of money, probably more than enough to reimburse all the ranchers from whom cattle and horses had been stolen. Moreover, the losses of any poor ranchers over on the Palouse range would have to be made good. That, however, could hardly make much of a hole in the fortune Mason had no doubt been accumulating for years.

The Indian came back from the barn, leading his horse. He sat down beside Dale and laid a heavy hand on his arm.

"No look! . . . Me see man watchin' on rock," he said.

"Where?" asked Dale, checking a start.

Nalook let go of Dale and curved a thumb that indicated the bare point on the west rim, in fact the only lookout on that side, and the one from which he had planned to get Rogers's signal. On the moment Rogers returned.

"Rogers, stand pat now," said Dale. "The Indian sighted someone watchin' us. From the bare point you know, where I was to come for our signal."

"Wal, thet ain't so good," growled the homesteader with concern. "Must be them cusses who busted through here, shootin'. By thunder, I'd like to get a crack at the feller who gave me this cut in the shoulder."

"I forgot, Rogers. Is it serious?"

"Not atall. But it's sore an' makes me sore. I was fool enough to show it to my wife. But I couldn't tie it up myself. Blood always sickens wimmen."

"What do?" asked the Indian.

"We won't let on we know we're bein' watched. . . . Rogers, could any scout on thet point see where you took your wife an' Edith?"

"I reckon not. Fact is, I'm not sure."

"Well, you stay here. It's reasonable to figure

these horse thieves won't come back. An' if any others came out of the valley, they'll be stretchin' leather. You keep hid. I'll take Nalook an' these men, an' see what's up out there."

"Couldn't do no better. But you want to come back by dark, 'cause thet girl begged me to tell you," replied Rogers earnestly. "Gosh, I never saw such eyes in a human's face. You be careful, Britt. Thet girl is jist livin' for you."

"Rogers, I'm liable to be so careful thet I'll be yellow," replied Dale soberly.

Soon Dale was jogging down the trail at the head of the quartet. In the brush cover at the outlet of the canyon they had to ride single file. Once out in the valley Nalook was the first to call attention to horses scattered here and there all over the green. They evidently had broken out of the pasture or had been freed. Dale viewed them and calculated their number with satisfaction. Not a rider in sight!

Dale led at a brisk trot. It did not take long to reach the lower trail. Here he sent Nalook up to fetch down the ten white men and three Indians that Strickland had been able to gather together. After an interval of keen survey of the valley, Dale voiced his surprise to Tom and Jason.

"Queer all right," agreed the older man. "Kinda feels like a lull before the storm."

"I wonder what happened to Stafford's outfit. They've had hours more time than needed. They've missed the trail."

The Indian was clever. He sent the men down on foot, some distance apart. They made but little noise and raised scarcely any dust. Dale looked this posse over keenly. They appeared to be mostly miners, rough, bearded, matured men. There were, however, several cowboys, one of whom Dale had seen at the horse sale. The last two to descend the trail proved to be Strickland with the Indian.

"By jove, you, Strickland!" ejaculated Dale, in surprise.

"I couldn't keep out of it, Brittenham," returned the rancher dryly. "This sort of thing is my meat. Besides, I'm pretty curious and sore."

"How about your cowboys?"

"I'm sure I can't understand why those outfits haven't shown up. But I didn't send for my own. I've only a few now and they're out on the range. Sanborn and Drew were to send theirs, with an outfit from the Circle Bar. Damn strange! This is stern range business that concerns the whole range."

"Maybe not so strange. If they were friends of Mason!"

"Thick as hops!" exclaimed Strickland with a snort.

"We'll go slow an' wait for Stafford's cowboys," decided Dale ponderingly.

"Hoss thieves all get away mebbe," interposed Nalook, plainly not liking this idea of waiting.

"All right, Nalook. What's your advice?"

"Crawl like Injun," he replied, and spread wide his fingers. "Mebbe soon shoot heap much."

"Strickland, this Indian is simply great. We'll be wise to listen to him. Take your men an' follow him. Cowboy, you hide here at the foot of the trail an' give the alarm if any riders come down. We've reason to believe some of the gang are scoutin' along this west rim. I'll slip up on top an' have a look at Mason's camp."

Drawing his rifle from its saddle sheath, Dale removed his coat and spurs. Nalook was already leading his horse into the brush, and the Indians followed him. Strickland, with a caustic word of warning to Dale, waved his men after the Indian.

"Come with me. Throw your chaps an' spurs, cowboy," advised Dale, and addressed himself to the steep trail. Soon the long-legged cowboy caught up with him, but did not speak until they reached the rim. Dale observed that he also carried a rifle and had the look of a man who could use it.

"Brittenham, if I see any sneakin' along the rim, shall I smoke 'em up?" he queried.

"You bet, unless they're cowboys."

"Wal, I shore know thet breed."

They parted. Dale stole into the evergreens, walking on his toes. He wound in and out, keeping as close to the rim as possible, and did not halt until he had covered several hundred yards. Then he listened and tried to peer over the rim. But he heard nothing and could see only the far part of the valley. Another quarter of a mile ought to put him where he could view Mason's camp. But he had not gone quite so far when a thud of hoofs on soft ground brought him up tight-skinned and cold. A horse was approaching a little distance from the rim. Dale glided out to meet it. Presently he saw a big sombero, then a red youthful face, above some evergreens. In another moment horse and rider came into view. Leveling his rifle, Dale called him to halt. The rider was unmistakably a young cowboy, and as cool as could be. He complied with some range profanity. Then at second glance he drawled, "Howdy, Brittenham."

"You've got the advantage of me, Mister Cowboy," retorted Dale curtly.

"Damn if I can see thet," he rejoined, with a smile that eased Dale's grimness.

"You know me?" queried Dale.

"Shore, I recognized you. I've a pard, Jen Pierce, who's helped you chase wild hosses. My name's Al Cook. We both ride for Stafford."

"You belong to Stafford's outfit?" asked Dale, lowering his rifle.

"Yep. We got heah before sunup this mornin'."

"How many of you an' where are they?"

"About twenty, I figger. Didn't count. Jud Larkin, our foreman, left five of us to watch thet far trail, up on top. He took the rest down."

"Where are they now?"

"I seen them just now. I can show them to you."

"Rustle. By gum, this *is* queer."

"You can gamble on it," returned Cook as he turned his horse. "We got tired waitin' for a showdown. I disobeyed orders an' rode around this side. Glad I did. For I run plumb across a trail fresh with tracks of a lot of horses. All shod! Brittenham, them hoss thieves have climbed out."

"Another trail? Hell! If thet's not tough.... Where is it?"

"Heads in thet deep notch back of them cabins."

"They had a back hole to their burrow. Nalook didn't know thet."

"Heah we air," said the cowboy, sliding off. "Come out on the rim."

In another moment Dale was gazing down upon the grove of pines and the roofs of cabins. No men—no smoke! The campsite appeared deserted.

"Say, what the hell you make of thet?" ejaculated the cowboy, pointing. "Look! Up behind the thicket, makin' for the open grass! There's Larkin's outfit all strung out, crawlin' on their bellies like snakes!"

Dale saw, and in a flash he surmised that Stafford's men were crawling up on Strickland's. Each side would mistake the other for the horse thieves. And on the instant a clear crack of a rifle rang out. But it was up on the rim. Other shots, from heavy short guns, boomed. That cowboy had run into the spying outlaws. Again the sharp ring of the rifle.

"Look!" cried the cowboy, pointing down.

Dale saw puffs of blue smoke rise from the green level below. Then gunshots pealed up.

"My Gawd! The locoed idiots are fighting each other. But at thet, neither Nalook or Strickland would know Stafford's outfit."

"Bad! Let me ride down an' put them wise."

"I'll go. Lend me your horse. You follow along the rim to the trail. Come down."

Dale ran back to leap into the cowboy's saddle. The stirrups fit him. With a slap of the bridle and a kick he urged the horse into a gallop. It did not take long to reach the trail. Wheeling into it, he ran the horse out to the rim, and then sent him down at a sliding plunge. He yelled to the cowboy on guard. "Brittenham! Brittenham! Don't shoot!" Then as the horse sent gravel and dust sky-high, and, reaching a level, sped by the cowboy, Dale added, "Look out for our men above!"

Dale ran the fast horse along the edge of the timber and then toward the thicket where he calculated Nalook would lead Strickland. He crashed through one fringe of sage and laurel, right upon the heels of men. Rifles cracked to left and right. Dale heard the whistle of bullets that came from Stafford's outfit.

"*Stop!*" he yelled, at the top of his lungs. "Horse thieves gone! You're fightin' our own men!"

Out upon the open grass level he rode, tearing loose his scarf. He held this aloft in one hand and in the other his rifle. A puff of white smoke rose from the deep grass ahead, then another from a clump of brush to the right, and next, one directly in front of him. The missile from the gun which belched that smoke hissed close to Dale's ear. He yelled with all his might and waved as no attacking enemy ever would have done. But the shots multiplied. The cowboys did not grasp the situation.

"No help for it!" muttered Dale with a dark premonition of calamity. But he had his good name to regain. He raced on right upon kneeling, lean-shaped cowboys.

"*Stop! Stop!* Horse thieves gone! You're fightin' friends! My outfit! Brittenham, Britt—"

Dale felt the impact of a bullet on his body somewhere. Then a terrible blinding shock.

When consciousness returned, Dale knew from a jolting sensation that he was being moved. He was being propped up in a saddle by a man riding on each side of his horse. His head sagged and when he opened his eyes to a blurred and darkened sight he saw the horn of his saddle and the mane of his horse. His skull felt as if it had been split by an ax.

His senses drifted close to oblivion again, then recovered a little more clearly. He heard voices and hoofbeats. Warm blood dripped down on his hands. That sensation started conscious thought. He had been shot, but surely not fatally, or he would not have been put astraddle a horse. His reaction to that was swift, and revivifying with happiness. A faintness, a dizziness seemed to lessen, but the pain in his head grew correspondingly more piercing.

Dale became aware then that a number of horsemen rode with him. They began to crash through brush out into the open again where gray walls restricted the light. Then he felt strong hands lift him from the saddle and lay him on the grass. He opened his eyes. Anxious faces bent over him, one of which was Strickland's.

"My Gawd, men!" came to Dale in Rogers's deep voice. "It's Brittenham! Don't say he's—"

"Just knocked out temporarily," replied Strickland cheerfully. "Ugly scalp wound, but not dangerous. Another shot through the left shoulder. Fetch whiskey, bandages, hot water, and iodine if you have it."

"Aw!" let out Rogers, expelling a loud breath. He thumped away.

Dale lay with closed eyes, deeply grateful for having escaped serious injury. They forced him to swallow whiskey, and then they began to work over him.

"You're the homesteader, Rogers?" asked Strickland.

"Yes. Me an' Britt have been friends. Knew each other over in the Sawtooths. . . . Lord, I'm glad he ain't bad hurt. It'd just have killed thet Watrous girl."

"I'm Strickland," replied the other. "These fellows here are part of a posse I brought up from Halsey."

"Much of a fight? I heerd a lot of shootin'."

"It would have been one hell of a fight but for Brittenham. You see, the horse-thief gang had vamoosed last night. But we didn't know that. The Indian led us up on an outfit that had discovered us about the same time. We were crawling toward each other, through the thickets and high grass. The Indians began to shoot first. That betrayed our position and a lively exchange of shots began. It grew hot. Brittenham had gone up on the rim to scout. He discovered our blunder and rode back hell-bent for election right into our midst. He stopped us, but the other outfit kept on shooting. Brittenham went on, and rode into the very face of hard shooting. He got hit twice. Nervy thing to do! But it saved lives. I had two men wounded besides him. Stafford's outfit suffered some casualties, but fortunately no one killed."

"What become of the hoss thieves?"

"Gone! After Reed and Mason had been killed, the gang evidently split. Some left in the night, leaving all their property except light packs. Sam Hood, one of Stafford's boys, killed two of them up on the rim, just before our fight started below."

"Ha! Thet ought to bust the gang for keeps," declared Rogers, rubbing his big hands.

"It was the best night's work this ranger ever saw. And the credit goes to Brittenham."

"Wal, I'll go fetch the wimmen," concluded Rogers heartily.

When, a little later, Dale had been washed and bandaged, and was half sitting up receiving the plaudits of the riders, he saw Edith come running out from under the trees into the open. She ran most of the way; then, nearing the cabin, she broke into a hurried walk and held a hand over her heart. Even at a distance Dale saw her big dark eyes, intent and staring in her pale face. As she neared the spot where he lay surrounded by a half-circle of strange men, it was certain she saw no one but him. Reaching the spot where he lay, she knelt beside him.

"Dale!"

"Hello—Edith," he replied huskily. "I guess I didn't bear such a charmed life—after all. I sure got in the way of two bullets. But my luck held, Edith."

"Oh! You're not seriously injured?" she asked composedly, with a gentle hand on his. "But you are suffering."

"My head did hurt like h—sixty. It's sort of whirlin' now."

"Rogers told me, Dale. That was a wonderful and splendid thing for you to do," Edith said softly. "What will Dad say? And won't I have Mister Stafford in a hole?"

Strickland interposed with a beaming smile. "You sure will, Miss Watrous. And I hope you make the most of it."

"Edith, I reckon we might leave for Bannock pronto," spoke up Dale eagerly. "I sent Nalook to tell your friends of your safety."

"Wal, Dale, mebbe I'll let you go tomorrow," chimed in Rogers.

"Don't go today," advised Strickland.

Next day Dale, despite his iron will and supreme eagerness to get home, suffered an ordeal that was almost too much for him. Toward the end of the ride to Bannock members of Strickland's posse were supporting Dale on his horse. But to his relief and Edith's poignant joy, he made it. At Bannock, medical attention and a good night's sleep made it possible for him to arrange to go on to Salmon by stage.

The cowboy Cook, who had taken a strong fancy to Dale, and had hung close to him, came out of the inn carrying a canvas-covered pack that Dale had him carefully stow under the seat.

"Britt, you sure have been keen about that pack. What's in it?" queried Strickland with shrewd curiosity.

"Wouldn't you like to know, old-timer?"

"I've got a hunch. Wal, I'll look you up over at the Watrous ranch in a couple of days. I want to go home first."

"Ahuh. You want to find out why those cowboy outfits didn't show up?"

"I confess to a little curiosity," replied the rancher dryly.

"Don't try to find out. Forget it," said Dale earnestly.

The stage, full of passengers, and driven by the

jovial stage driver Bill Edmunds, rolled away to the cheers of a Bannock crowd.

"Dale, what *is* in this pack under the seat?" asked Edith.

"Guess."

"It looked heavy, and considering how fussy you've been about it—I'd say—*gold*," she whispered.

Dale put his lips to her ear. "Edith, no wonder I'm fussy. I'm wild with excitement. That gang is broken up. An' I have Reed's money in my coat here—an' Mason's fortune in thet pack."

"Oh, how thrilling!" she whispered, and then on an afterthought she spoke out roguishly. "Well, in view of the—er—rather immediate surrender of your independence, I think I'd better take charge."

Darkness had settled down over the Salmon River Valley when the stage arrived at Salmon. Old Bill, the driver, said to Edith, "I reckon I'd better hustle you young folks out home before the town hears what Britt has done."

"That'd be good of you, Bill," replied Edith gratefully. "Dale is tired. And I'd be glad to get him home pronto."

They were the only passengers for the three miles out to the ranch. Dale did not speak, and Edith appeared content to hold his hand. They both gazed out at the shining river and the dark groves, and over the moonlit range. When they arrived at the ranch, Dale had Bill turn down the lane to the little cabin where he lived.

"Carry this pack in, Bill, an' don't ask questions, you son-of-a-gun, or you'll not get the twenty-dollar gold piece I owe you."

"Wal, if this hyar pack is full of gold, you won't miss thet double eagle, you doggone lucky wild-hoss hunter."

"Thank you, Bill," said Edith. "I'll walk the rest of the way."

Dale was left alone with Edith, who stood in the shadow of the maples with the moon lighting her lovely face. He could hear the low roar of rapids on the river.

"It's wonderful, gettin' back, this way," he said haltingly. "You must run in an' tell your dad."

"Dad can wait a moment longer. . . . Oh, Dale, I'm so proud—so happy—my heart is bursting."

"Mine feels queer, too. I hope this is not a dream, Edith."

"What—Dale?"

"Why, all thet's happened—an' you standin' there safe again—an' so beautiful. You just don't appear real."

"I should think you could ascertain whether I'm real flesh and blood or not."

Dale fired to that. "You'll always be the same, Edith. Can't you see how serious this is for me?" He took her in his arms. "Darlin', I reckon I know how you feel. But no words can tell you my feelins. . . . Kiss me, Edith—then I'll try."

She was in his arms, to grow responsive and loving in her eager return of his kisses.

"Oh—Dale!" she whispered, with eyes closed. "I have found my man at last."

"Edith, I love you—an' tomorrow I'll have the courage to ask your dad if I can have you."

"Dale, I'm yours—Dad or no Dad. But he'll be as easy as that," she replied, stirring in his arms and snapping her fingers. "I hate to leave you. But we have tomorrow—and forever. Oh, Dale! I don't deserve all this happiness—kiss me good night. . . . I'll fetch your breakfast myself. . . . Kiss me once more. . . . Another! Oh, I am—"

She broke from him to run up the lane and disappear under the moonlit maples. Dale stood there a few moments alone in the silver-blanched gloom, trying to persuade himself that he was awake and in possession of his senses.

Next morning he got up early, to find the pain in his head much easier. But his shoulder was so stiff and sore that he could not use the arm on that side. Having only one hand available, he was sore beset by the difficulty of washing, shaving, and making himself as presentable as possible. He did not get through any too soon, for Edith appeared up the lane accompanied by a servant carrying a tray. She saw him and waved, then came tripping on. Dale felt his heart swell and he moved about to hide his tremendous pride. He shoved a bench near the table under a canvas shelter that served for a porch. And when he could look up again, there she was, radiant in white.

"Mornin', Edith. Now I believe in fairies again."

"Oh, you look just fine. I'm having my breakfast with you. Do you feel as well as you look?"

"Okay, except for my arm. It's stiff. I had a devil of a time puttin' my best foot forward. You'll have to do with a one-armed beau today."

"I'd rather have your one arm than all the two arms on the range," she replied gaily.

They had breakfast together, which to Dale seemed like enchantment. Then she took him for a stroll under the cottonwoods out along the river bank. And there, hanging on his good arm, she told him how her father had taken her story. Visitors from Salmon had come last night up to a late hour, and had begun to arrive already that morning. Stafford's outfit had returned driving a hundred recovered horses. Dale's feat was on the tip of every tongue.

"I didn't tell Dad about—about *us* till this morning," she added finally.

"Lord help me! What'd he say?" gulped Dale.

"I don't know whether it was flattering—or not—to me," Edith replied dubiously. "He said, 'That wild-horse tamer? Thank God, your hash is settled at last!' "

"He sure flatters me if he thinks I can tame you. Wait till I tell him how you routed Bayne's outfit!"

"Oh, Dale, Dad was fine. He's going to ask you . . . But that'd be telling."

"Edith, if he accepts me, must I—will I have to wait very long for you?"

"*If!* Dad has accepted you, Dale. And honestly, he's happy over it. . . . And as for the other—just what do you mean, Mr. Brittenham?"

"Aw! Will you marry me soon?"

"How soon?"

"I—I don't know, darlin'."

"Dale, dearest, I couldn't marry you with your head bandaged like that—or your arm in a sling," she said tantalizingly, as her dark eyes shed soft warm light upon them.

"But, Edith!" he burst out. "I could take them off pronto. In less than a week!"

"Very well. Just that pronto."

Watrous came out to meet them as they crossed the green. His fine face showed emotion and his eyes, at that moment, had something of the fire of Edith's. He wrung Dale's hand. But as befitted a Westerner, little trace of his deep feeling pervaded his voice.

"Brittenham, I won't try to thank you," he said in simple heartiness.

"Thet suits me, Mr. Watrous. I'm kind of overwhelmed. An'—so I'd better get somethin' out before I lose my nerve. . . . I've loved Edith since I came here first, three years ago. Will you give her to me?"

"Dale, I will, and gladly, provided you live here

with me. I'm getting on, and since Mother has been gone, Edith has been all to me."

"Dad, we will never leave you," replied Edith softly.

"Bless you, my children! And Dale, there's a little matter I'd like to settle right now. I'll need a partner. Stafford has persuaded me to go in big for the cattle game. I see its possibilities. That, of course, means we'll have cattle stealing as we have had horse stealing. I'll need you pretty bad."

"Dad!" cried Edith in dismay. "You didn't tell me you'd want Dale to go chasing cattle thieves!"

"My dear, it might not come for years. Such developments come slowly. By that time Dale may have grown some cowboy sons to take his place."

"Oh!" exclaimed Edith, plunged into sudden confusion.

"Dale, do you accept?" added Watrous, extending his hand with an engaging smile.

"Yes, Mr. Watrous. An' I'll give Edith an' you the best thet's in me."

"Settled! Oh, here comes Stafford. Lay into him, youngster, for he sure has been nasty."

As Stafford came slowly down the broad steps, Dale found himself unable to feel the resentment that had rankled in him.

"Brittenham," said the rancher, as he advanced, "I've made blunders in my life, but never so stupid a one as that regarding you. I am ashamed and sorry. It'll be hard for me to live this injustice down unless you forgive me. Can I ask that of you?"

"Nothin' to forgive," declared Dale earnestly, won by Stafford's straightforwardness and remorse. He offered his hand and gripped the rancher's. "Suspicion pointed at me. An' I took on Hildrith's guilt for reasons you know. Let's forget it an' be friends."

"You are indeed a man."

But when Stafford turned to Edith he had a different proposition to face. She eyed him with disdainful scorn, and stood tapping a nervous foot on the path.

"Edith, you can do no less than he. Say you forgive me, too."

"Yes, of course, since Dale is so kind. But I think you are a rotten judge of men."

"Indeed I am, my dear."

"And you're a hard man when you're crossed."

"Yes. But I'm a loyal friend. After all, this was a misunderstanding. You believed it, didn't you?"

"I never did—not for a minute. That's why I followed Dale."

"Well, you found him and brought him back." Stafford took a colored slip of paper from his pocket. He looked at it, then held it out to Edith. "I offered five thousand dollars reward for Brittenham, dead or alive. You brought him back alive—very much alive, as anyone with half an eye could see. And no wonder! It seems to me that this reward should go to you. Indeed, I insist upon your taking it."

"Reward! But, Mr. Stafford—you—I," stammered Edith. "Five thousand dollars for *me*?"

"Surely. I imagine you will be able to spend it pronto. We all know your weakness for fine clothes and fine horses. Please accept it as a wedding present from a friend who loves you and who will never cease to regret that he mistook so splendid and noble a fellow as Dale Brittenham for a horse thief!"